In a Maze of Imagination

A Novel

Kacy Cooney

This is a work of fiction. Names, characters, places, and incidents either are the product of the author's imagination or are used fictitiously, and any resemblance to actual persons, living or dead, business establishments, events, or locales is entirely coincidental.

to honor the memory of
Lena Forsyth

ACKNOWLEDGMENTS

Thank you to my aunt, Byra Cooney Schworer for allowing me to use my cousin Peter Schworer's amazing artwork for the cover.
I am also grateful to Amy Perina, Will Lahneman, and all the various members of the TJ writers group who have given me encouragement and useful feedback as this work went through the editing process.
To my family, Gerald and Roxanne, thank you for your love and patience.

Also by Kacy Cooney:
Seeking Solace

I had one weekend to make up my mind
if I didn't lose it first.

CHAPTER ONE

I had been to Lofton Beach only once before, when
I was eight years old and my mother had run out of
excuses to give Aunt Chris for why I couldn't spend a
week of my summer holiday with my cousins at the
beach. It was an opportunity my sister Joella never had.
She was too young, just a baby the time I went, and
though I suspect my aunt continued to offer invitations,
I knew nothing of them.

I felt very grown up that week, going off with my
aunt's family. My saucy, know-it-all cousins had
included me in their games and treated me as well as
they treated each other. We ran around in the acres of
sand dunes, bodysurfed in the smaller waves, and built
sandcastles when the waves were too strong for
swimming. It had been a week of marvelous freedom.
We girls had had a room of our own at the one story
motor lodge, while my aunt, uncle, and the boys had
slept in the room next door. Aunt Chris had usually
cooked supper on the hibachi in the parking lot, like
many of the other guests, and every evening a party
erupted among the various families. Dozens of children
ran loose about the town and the dunes, keeping away
from the dangers of the ocean.

I still treasured the memories of that most tranquil week, which may have been the reason I chose to return now. That and listening to bits and pieces of chatter all day yesterday between the shop manicurist and her clientele about trips to Hilton Head and cruises in the Caribbean. Hearing about their escapes made me long for one too.

So here I was, Carmen Trahan, taking advantage of my Sunday to Monday weekend to decide the future of my family. I had given myself until tomorrow afternoon, when I got on the bus back to Eastmont to settle our fates. I was less fearful of rushing into the wrong decision than I was of allowing it to drag on and drag me down.

So here I was in Lofton Beach again after seventeen years. It had grown faster than I had. Most of the low lying inns were gone, replaced by grand, tall structures like the Neptune Hotel, where I was staying this weekend. The beach was still wide and pale, with its pristine acres of tall dunes and vales.

I'd taken the last bus last night. I'd arrived in the early hours, between the nap on the bus and the longer nap in my luxurious room. After a breakfast of peanut butter crackers from the floor's snack machine, I dressed for the beach. I'd lost my water bottle on the bus, so I bought a bottle of water from the drink machine before I left the cool building. The day was already bright and hot. Eager to find privacy, I strayed from the wooden walkway to the shore and roamed the dunes until I found a spot with a couple of scrawny shade trees and nothing else. I couldn't see another person or the ocean, but I could hear it occasionally. The place was perfect.

Spreading my mat under the trees, I smiled again at Robert's little joke. He was the owner of the shop where I worked and my conspirator, along with our shopping savvy receptionist, in arranging this getaway. When I'd discovered that I needed a credit card to make a reservation, he had used his to pay for the room in advance (I had already repaid him for most of it). He was pleased that I was making plans, even if I wasn't actually going to take the vacation from work that he'd been telling me I needed to take for the last couple of months. "It's a start, Carmen. Now, I'm going to check you for tan lines when you come back!" In his prissy, jovial tone he had implied that he expected me to sunbathe in the nude. He wasn't serious, so I wasn't offended. We both knew very well—both being red heads and professional beauticians—that the best possible outcome of sitting in the sun was a new batch of freckles. With greater sincerity, he concluded with, "Be daring."

That was advice I could try to follow. Leaving town was a good start, but I knew that he was right to suggest that I do something other people considered risky. I liked the idea because I could use it as a distraction that might postpone my thinking about the real decision I needed to make.

My spot was so isolated that I wasn't likely to be arrested for stripping, but I had never liked exposing myself. I sat and lifted my dress off over my head. I scrounged through my bag for the sun screen, though I'd covered myself before I dressed. I wanted to be ready to add another layer in case some had rubbed off. I thought about how I would feel if I took Robert's suggestion and someone came wandering through my little valley to find me. I pushed away the vision of an angry man ogling me, and transformed him into an amiable older fellow walking beside his sunburned wife. They smiled at each other, remembering what it was like to be twenty-five. Next I pictured a fortyish woman coming along, carrying a picnic lunch for her large family. She smiled at me too, wistfully thinking how she had gone to a nude beach with the man she didn't marry until she pictured her own daughter in my place. Her voice would be just a little sharp when she said, "Your little, white breasts are going to get a horrid sunburn." And I knew what the young men I refused to picture would say: "She sure doesn't have the body for it," as they sped by lobbing a volleyball between them.

If I had intended to take Robert's dare, those phantoms would have dissuaded me. Today was all about taking chances, but I couldn't see how humiliating myself would give me the confidence I needed to face my questions. There was enough to do without distracting myself, and as yet that was all I had managed to do. If a few hours on a beach was all I needed to think clearly I could have gone to one of the beaches closer to Eastmont at a good deal less trouble and expense. I could have made a trip out to the lake on Friday night. I could have already dealt with this.

But I had turned my purpose into procrastination. I'd traveled on a whim, taking a first-rate trip, looking for unbiased solitude in order to contemplate the fate of my family. I'd come too far and invested too much to go home without giving my sister the benefit of the fair consideration that I had promised her. I owed her that much, though she had asked for help I wasn't sure I could give.

I reached over to get a drink of water as a way to cool the heat from all of the bottled frustration I felt. It was turning warm already. Maybe the morning was as hot as it felt. As I unscrewed the cap, bubbles rushed to the top, hissing and fizzing sideways, trying to come out before I completely removed the cap. Water sprayed me, and I started to retighten the lid as I read the label: seltzer water. Instead of agonizing over a vending machine error, I stretched my arms and shoulders, literally shrugging off the tension mistakes like this brought me, so that I wouldn't waste all of the time I had.

At the moment I was angry at my little sister. This whole predicament was Joella's fault, and she knew it. She had apologized, but she was not penitent. She was asking too much, yet she was my little sister. I must treat her fairly.

I wanted clarity, which is why I had removed myself from all the persuasive voices of home, yet now the first clear thought that I had was that I needed some solid advice. So, who would I have talked to if I had stayed home to talk to someone? Who did I know who would listen? Whose advice could I trust?

While I thought, I twirled my hair in my fingers. Some of my old friends, high school friends like Arlene or Rosa, might understand well enough to help me, but we hadn't stayed close. And newer friends wouldn't understand. I didn't want to explain why I had to struggle over this. I'd lose their respect and their friendship.

It was clear that my best option was to consult a professional, and before I had a chance to mourn my inability to afford that kind of help I realized that I did know someone in whom I could confide. If I could get the words out, if I had stayed home instead of running off as I had, I should have gone to see Father Oleg Fuentes, the youth leader at my church. He had studied a lot of psychology and he was trained to help people with all kinds of problems. And I knew him well enough. I was even comfortable with him. He was one of my customers; I'd washed his hair, evened his sideburns, and had many discussions with him at my workplace or his. And all of them had remained pleasant and neutral, even when they had been substantive. He was the right person for me to talk to. I felt certain that I could trust him to have my best interests at heart.

"Well," I said to myself, "What would I say to Father Oleg if I was talking to him now?" I didn't answer my question. The truth of it was that I wanted to discuss this even less than I wanted to think about it, and I quickly began trying to come up with another stall tactic. Except there just weren't any more.

"That's it then, I guess," I said to myself. "I'm not clever enough to come up with another distraction. I'll have to think about Joella now."

"What about Joella?" a man's voice said into my left ear.

I jumped, turning my head to see the person I knew as not there. I had already identified the voice, sluggish and thin. As one part of my mind lost patience with the rest of it, I had pulled Father Oleg out of my repressed but vivid imagination, and he leaned forward into view, seated beside me. Just the man I thought I could talk to, except that he was a projection of me, and I had plenty of doubts about how useful he would be even if he wasn't sharing my thoughts.

"Carmen? What's going on?" he asked with an air of having been pulled, for real, from his morning meeting with the guidance counselors at the church school to this plot of desert. His head pivoted around taking in the landscape. "Where are we? And where the hell is the ocean?"

"Lofton Beach, and the ocean is that way," I replied, pointing.

His olive skin was flushed. His expression was strained. "Why are we in Lofton Beach? Did you change shops? Will you still cut my hair?"

"No. I'll be back at Georges on Tuesday. I just, well…" I couldn't explain.

"I see," he nodded. "So? What is going on?"

"I just needed some quiet to think properly."

"Looks like you've got some. Except for pulling me out of thin air like you did. You know I don't do quiet very well." He looked around, still somewhat annoyed. "Killer spot you found. Shade, a view—well, sort of—a healthy walk to the water. If you had a breeze, it might be pleasant."

"You're here."

He laughed. "With my breezy personality. Now everything's perfect." He pointed at my skull. "Of course, I'm only in there."

I shrugged.

"Would you mind changing me into something a little more appropriate for the beach? How can I go swimming in all these heavy clothes?"

I cringed at the idea seeing him in swimwear, but without further thought clad him in lightweight khakis and the black *Jesus Christ Superstar* t-shirt the teens had given him that had a little white square sewn into the ribbing on the collar. "Better?"

"Yeah, thanks." He changed the subject. "Are you growing out your hair? Seems longer."

"Yes."

"Doesn't that go against some kind of hairstylists' code of ethics? You ladies always have such spiffy dos."

I laughed. "Overworked hair? Yes. It's a hazard of the trade."

"Now, I don't suppose you fetched me all the way here for a fashion consult. I'm hardly so qualified as nearly every girl you know." He was taking a nice, gentle way to approach the serious subject, one of the reasons that I had summoned him, I suppose.

Or maybe it was because I actually did have some control over him and I still didn't want to get down to business. I made myself admit, "I need advice, Father."

"Aha! Good. I was hoping you'd get to it before you decided to go in for lunch."

"You'll come with me, won't you?" I said with an eagerness I didn't expect to feel.

"Sure. I'll come to watch you trying to discuss this whatever it is that you don't want to discuss in front of all the people who will be staring at you because you're talking to the empty seat across the table."

"Good point. Thanks. I knew there was a reason I chose to consult you."

"So: out with it."

"Joella is pregnant."

"Oh my. That's a bundle of news." He paused to flip the leather thongs off his feet into the sand a yard or so away. He must have decided that he would be staying for a while. "How are your folks taking the news?"

"Actually, Jo hasn't told them yet. That's one of the things, telling them, she wants me to help her do. You know my folks well enough to know that she's got to be prepared. And honestly, so must I."

"Go on. Explaining things, even if it is really only to yourself, will help you work them out."

"Alright, Father. I hope so. Jo is almost eighteen and just started her senior year of high school, and she's at least two months pregnant. Her boyfriend, a boy named Justin, graduated last year and enlisted in the Army. He's in training now, but he'll probably end up in Afghanistan. He doesn't know about the baby yet. She doesn't have any idea how he will handle the news. First love. God! They're so young."

"That's right, you are seven years her senior," he said in a condescending tone.

"It's a major seven years," I countered.

I had built a new life in the years since high school. Desperate as I was to move out, I had waited four months. It took that long to find a little apartment I could afford to share with some other girls. I worked two jobs, but I never told any of my family that I'd moved on from the fast food place where I'd worked since I was sixteen. I hid my earnings from my father so that he wouldn't demand that I pay more rent, which he collected from me though my mother received a government subsidy because of her disability. Once I moved out I didn't tell them where I lived or worked or that I'd enrolled in Beauty College. It took a couple of years for me to trust Joella with more than the telephone number that I had given to our parents to permit contact.

"I gather she wants to raise the baby with or without Justin, but she believes deep down that he'll be eager to marry her and love this child."

"Of course she does, but she won't admit it. She's asked me to help her. To let her live with me mainly, but I'm sure she'll need a lot more than that from me."

"And?"

"And I don't know what to do." I folded my arms over my chest and lowered my head so I could rest my chin on my fist.

"Why would you not choose to help your sister, Carmen?" he asked. It was an intellectual inquiry, without a hint of emotion or judgment.

"Because." Did I want to tell him that I thought she was taking advantage of me? That I thought she was making a huge mistake, and that I didn't want to be a part of it? "Our parents, Oleg," I said at last, unable to remain silent while his unblinking eyes bored into me. "What she's done will upset them so much."

"How much?"

"She's always pushed the limits, and they've always had to be strict with her. Now, I'm afraid they'll kick her butt right out the door, and mine with her if I stand up for her."

"If that's the way they feel, why not let them do just that?"

"Who will take care of them? They need us. They need at least one of us to help them. They aren't healthy, and as they get older it will only get worse.

They won't let anyone but Jo and me help them. I already worry about them. How can I help them, if they disown me?"

"I didn't think you had much to do with them."

"I look in on them fairly often." It was a bit of an exaggeration. I tried to visit about every other week.

"So you feel you must choose between your sister and your parents?"

I guess he understood my predicament as well as I did. A real person would probably still be confused. "Pretty much. Except that Jo is stronger than they are. She's resilient. She can probably manage on her own, eventually, or someone else might step in to help her."

"She's a child, bearing a child, Carmen. Who would you trust to help her?"

"Joella has more options than my parents do," I grumbled.

"And she's more forgiving than your parents. She won't hate you if you let her down." He wasn't looking at me anymore. His eyes were focused on the blue sky above the dune in front of us, his hands wrapped around his bent knee holding himself in an upright position, with his other leg, the left one, the one that had been mangled during a construction accident about twenty years before, as flat as it could go on the ground. A breeze kicked in and played with his hair. He didn't seem to notice that either. I felt like I was the imagined presence, that he was more real than I, and I wished very hard for him to acknowledge me.

At last, still gazing at the distant sky, he spoke again. "Look, Carmen, if I didn't know what you know, if I really were Oleg Fuentes trying to advise you, I'd have to say that I don't know your parents well and that what I do know about them isn't terribly good. Since I do know what you know, I can tell you aren't gaining much from your continued association with them."

I stared at him, my mouth fallen open. My imagination seemed truly to have stumped me this time.

"Things might work out for Joella." I didn't realize that he had continued speaking until after his words sunk into my thoughts. "I admire your desire to be a good daughter," he said more soothingly.

"I try," I said quietly.

"Are you one?"

"Sometimes, and sometimes not. Have you always been a good son?"

"Probably not, but if I asked my mama and papa, I know they'd say, 'Yes,' that I had *always* been a good son. What do you think your parents would say? Don't you think they could overlook what I will for the moment call Joella's mistake? Do you think they will be so angry that they won't continue to love her and love her child despite all the circumstances?"

"They won't overlook it. They won't forgive her."

"Don't you think they know they need you? Are they stupid enough to throw away the only people in the world who care about them?"

I shrugged. It was a sensible argument, but I really couldn't answer his questions.

"I think you're making this into a more difficult choice than you need to, Carmen. I doubt it's an all or nothing deal."

"But they do need us," I returned. My eyes were wet, and my voice cracked, whining, even pleading. "How can I desert them? Joella is stronger, she is more capable, and though I may prefer to help her, she is the one who started this."

"She's just a kid, Carmen. Do you really think she knew much better?"

"She should. She's been taught. She got into trouble for breaking her curfew. She's been grounded. Hell, she was grounded when she got pregnant!"

"She's in love for the first time with a young man leaving home to be a soldier, *in wartime*. Don't you think that might make a girl a little reckless?"

I picked up the water bottle and began to play with the cap while I considered his question. He was quiet. He may have even disappeared briefly while I wished I had not left my magazine in my room. Then I thought again about why I had come here, and I noticed Oleg in my peripheral vision stretching his arms and legs.

"You don't understand her, do you?" he broke the silence.

"No. I've never been in love."

"Not at all?"

"No. Not yet."

"Damn."

"And you know all about it?" I asked him.

"Me? No." He shook his head. "You won't believe this, but I wasn't always as cool as I am now. I liked plenty of girls, but I don't think I knew how to make the right kind of impression. And if it's all one-sided, it doesn't count. But I think I know something of how it might feel. And I've had a chance to observe lots of other people when they're in love." He smiled. "And I don't mean the goofy stuff they do. I mean the real things, important things like making homes and wanting to have children, because their hearts are overflowing.   Your sister may have gone through something very wonderful, though she probably wasn't prepared."

I felt a wave of sadness and envy.   I couldn't imagine letting myself get so lost in another person that I would be willing to risk everything to make him happy.   She must have been made differently than I was.

"Now, if you can set aside your biases and cynicism, Carmen, how involved do you think the father of this baby will be?"

"I only know what Joella has told me."

"It would be convenient to know what my real world counterpart knows at this point about Justin.   Did he go to our church?   Was he in the youth group?"

"I think so," I replied shrugging.

He sighed.   "So, let's say that he won't be very involved.   Worst case scenario."   His manner was formal.   "Will she have to sue him for support?"

"I don't know.   I don't think so.   I mean, he sounds decent and like he comes from a nice family.   They tried to do a lot of things for Joella.   That's part of the reason that she ended up in trouble all the time with our parents.   His were always inviting her over, and ours never wanted her to go."

"Do you think she could go to his parents for help?"

I stared down at my bent knees.   The sun was moving into my shady area, and I would have to move soon.   I thought hard about how to answer this question, my own distrust trying to prevail over my gut feelings. "Yes," I said at last and let out a large breath.

"Is Joella corresponding with Justin?"

"I don't know…probably."

With a knowing chuckle, he said, "They are both sure to grow up a good deal in these next months."

"Amen."

He scrunched his face and said, "That's my line."

"Okay. Fine. Then you say it."

"Amen."

CHAPTER TWO

Father Oleg and I wasted a few minutes wishing we knew more about Justin. "It would help if I'd met him," I said, thinking this was another reason to have stayed at home and talked to Joella.

"You need to sort out your feelings."

"Okay," I said emotionlessly. "But I'm not one of those people who blubbers out all of their thoughts before they go through my brain."

"Even so, you seem to be making good use of this talk it out approach. You must have used it before."

Nodding, I replied, "It's never been quite so visual before."

He reached out his hand, but his arm was not quite long enough to give me a sympathetic pat. As he leaned forward, his arm became shorter, keeping his hand at an unbroken distance. I toyed with this new power briefly before he broke into my thoughts again, "It forces you think twice about everything you say."

"What about what you say?"

"Three times when I speak. Four when you answer me."

"This is weird."

"I don't know about that. You'd be surprised how frequently I appear in women's fantasies."

"You need to develop some self-confidence, Father."

He laughed. "We all have our idiosyncrasies. Even you."

"Don't I know it?" I looked around. "I mean look at me now. Look at me looking at you."

"You think therefore I am."

"You must be my intellectual side."

"I'm glad you have one, but couldn't I be on your fun side? At least for a little while?"

"I've been told I don't have a fun side."

"That is a problem for another day." He leaned back, stretching out on my mat and encroaching into my space.

"Excuse me!"

"You're supposed to go swimming."

"That is probably the best advice I'll get all day," I replied. "But I really ought to address my sister's problem."

"You aren't doing much about it now, Carmen. So you might as well cool off and relax and see what pops into your head."

"You popped into my head." I caught him sneering at me. "That's kind of frightening, Father Gargoyle." I shook my head and rose straight up from my cross legged position. "You've convinced me to go."

"Don't get into any trouble," he said casually, as I got my towel out of my bag.

Figuring that everything he said had some kind of Freudian hidden meaning, I snapped, "What are you suggesting?"

He cringed and threw his hands up to guard his face like he was expecting a blow. "Well, you've run off and all that. I just thought you might try to do something stupid. To be like your sister. So you'll get kicked out of the family together." He was more devious than I expected. I guess I don't quite know the depths of my own mind.

"I'm not overly fond of the idea of getting kicked out of the family for *being good* to my sister."

He nodded. "Practical. Why bother getting punished for doing the right thing when you can just as easily be punished for doing something wrong? It's the kind of logic I would have used, except my parents didn't waste their time with unnecessary discipline."

"They sound like sensible people."

"They are. And you," he cocked his head. "You planning to get pregnant too?"

What a repulsive idea! I played sassy with him anyway. "Could be."

"Seriously?" His interest piqued.

"No." I let out a heavy sigh. "Definitely not. Don't think I want to pass along my DNA."

He didn't reply. I was afraid as soon as I said it that he would jump on that remark. Partly to make sure he didn't do so belatedly, I announced that I was going to go for the aforementioned swim. I slung my towel over one shoulder, asking, "Can you reach your stuff?"

"None of it's real, remember. But if you want, go on and picture it all right at my side."

I couldn't help but laugh when his cane and sandals were instantly transported to a more convenient location. "I don't suppose we are all just living in the imagination of some greater being?"

"Think that's how we got started."

"Yeah. I guess that would be your professional opinion." I started to walk away. I glanced back over my shoulder, hoping to see only my belongings, but Oleg was still there, looking inland, and I let the dune rise between us before I had to see what he was watching. If he wouldn't disappear, then I must. I kept walking.

The wind was strong, fresh, and cooling, counteracting the brightness of the sun. I had to squint hard to see my way to the water, but as soon as I was ankle deep, tenseness began to ease out of my muscles. While I hadn't realized I had been carrying so much stress I was thankful that I could let it go, and I enjoyed those carefree moments, playing in the surf, knowing that my imagination was carrying on just fine without me there to direct it.

I'm not certain what I expected to do this weekend. I had promised to decide whether or not to help my sister, but I really hadn't thought further along than getting away from everyone involved. I had thought that it would be easier to consider things objectively if I didn't have anyone around me trying to persuade me of anything. It may have seemed like I expected the sand and saltwater to lend me wisdom, but I did know better. Under the best of circumstances I needed privacy to feel brave, and I needed courage to stop vacillating and punishing myself.

I was almost dry by the time I returned to my mat. The sand on my feet and ankles was crumbling, and I was thinking about going in to get something refreshing to drink. I was definitely not expecting to see anyone, not really even the intrepid Father Oleg, but not only was he still there, but Justin was with him. From this distance I could only distinguish that he was dressed in military uniform fatigues.

Then I noticed my sister standing near them, her eyes fixed expectantly on me, her belly bulging like she was ready to drop full-term triplets. And my parents lurked a few feet away. My father leaned forward threateningly over the scene. My mother's lips moved, emitting caustic sounds in Joella's direction.

Joella looked nauseous, but not as intimidated as I felt at that moment. Father Oleg defied my father by remaining conciliatory and attempting to mediate. He took a step toward my parents, and my mother turned her bulk and her vicious temper on him, pushing him to the ground where Oleg remained due to his restricted mobility. He didn't even try to rise, but shifted into a more dignified, seated position, and continued trying to inject some calm and kindness into my phantom kinsfolk.

Not knowing Justin and unwilling to grant him any unproven virtues, I left him hanging back. A fixed smile was on his face, which I had seen once in a photograph. He was merely an extra in my family drama, just a static presence.

The more my mother ranted, the straighter Joella stood, as if the threats only made her stronger. There was no time to wonder why I pictured her that way. As real as everything seemed, Oleg was the most real to me, perhaps because he was the only one I had invited. When I got close enough, I offered him a hand to help him to his feet. He nodded his thanks, his face expressing sympathy, apology, and disgust all at once. "Sorry," he whispered. "Things got out of hand all the sudden. I was actually having a good talk with Justin. Then they popped up and…"

"I'm afraid that's my fault, Father." Of course it was. There was no one else to blame for any of the activity around me.

My mother hadn't noticed me before, but as soon as she did, she attacked. "What's your part in this?"

"I just dreamed this up," I said simply explaining this meeting rather than its purpose.

"That's not what I meant, girl," she snapped, her mouth working. Her flaccid jowls shook over the flexing of the muscles in her cheeks. "How long have you known about your sister's problem?" Her bloodshot eyes bored into my courage.

"Her problem?" Even in my imagination I felt the need to be cautious. My mother could pick one word from among dozens to find fault. She was relentless. My father was quiet. They were the kind of opposites that completed each other. She hated him, but she would never have dared to speak ill of him.

"I know that Joella told you she's pregnant. Don't try to deny it. I know what you know." This was something that my mother said frequently when trying to obtain details of private issues. Today, for a change, it was true.

"She told me Friday."

"Friday? It's Sunday," my mother said in mock shock. "When were you going to tell me?"

"And you," Dad turned on Joella, "why were you telling your sister about this before us? Hmm?"

"It was easier to talk to her," she said quietly, her voice steady. She glanced at me and then to Justin. She was holding up well, though her belly seemed to be growing. Maybe she had learned to withstand their spite better than I had.

My mother shook her head with disapproval. "You kids." Having nothing to say, she didn't bother to complete her sentence. It didn't weaken her position. Nothing ever did, but still she seemed to shrink just a little.

"You're damned right to be shaking in your shoes, young lady," Dad began. He was talking to one or both of us, but I couldn't tell which. He didn't seem to be plugged into my memory center the way the others were. That was realistic.

"Little slut," my mother interjected.

"We've let you get away with too much," he went on, paying no attention to Mom. "Bah, staying out late with that snotty nosed boy." He pointed at Justin, his head down and forward like a butting ram. "And now he's gone off and left you. Deserted you and made sure to drag our family's reputation through the muck. It's your own fucking fault. You're on your own. Yes, that's right, on your own! We won't bail you out of this predicament."

"See what you've done, Joella. I raised you better than this. No one will trust you now." Mom seemed to expand again.

I glanced at Joella. She looked so small, still a little girl in so many ways. I realized that Oleg was right. She was caught up in her first love. She had been sorrowful and overly dramatic about her boyfriend's likely departure for the War on Terror. I had no doubt that he loved her too, but eighteen and nineteen year old boys don't often think about the consequences of sex. They just want it. And with so many conflicting pressures a naïve girl would want to make her boyfriend happy. She would give too much of herself without thinking past her idyllic desires to the possible consequences. I felt a sudden, strong urge to protect her.

As I reached to take Jo's hand, my father stepped between us, towering over us. He pushed us apart roughly. Jo stumbled. "No more of this," he sneered. "The two of you in cahoots. You've got to stop it now, or you'll both end up out on the streets. Two whores! You've made so much trouble for me."

"We've done everything we could for you girls. We've done our best," Mom began. She sounded reasonable; this trick had often lulled us into her guilt trap.

"I know," I replied cautiously, but in a soothing tone.

"This is tearing apart our family. Nothing's more important than taking care of each other." The words sounded as fatigued as my mother looked.

"How will the family help Joella?" I asked.

Of course, I couldn't even imagine her answer to this question. She just repeated another familiar phrase, "We should discuss this privately, Carmen," she said. She glanced quickly toward Justin, Father Oleg, and perhaps even Joella. I couldn't supply her with a further argument. I had never asked her to explain her views before. "Barney, there are too many people here. Don't you think we should have our discussion when there aren't any strangers around?" She stared at me with her eyes narrowed. "We'll resume this conversation later."

My dad had no time to respond before they disappeared, leaving me wishing I could have said a few more things to them now while their arguments were not fully prepared, though I knew that it would only be practice. If I had my way, I wouldn't see either of my folks again until I had to, but then it would be real and they would have all of their weapons at hand to use against Joella and me.

Joella slowly looked up from the spot on the ground where our mother had stood. Her eyes rested on me for a moment before she turned to Justin. Only he could answer her biggest questions. He held hope and despair for her, but she didn't know how much of either. I turned to watch him too. He was talking to Oleg again, but we could hear nothing more than the muted surf. Oleg patted him on the back and began to direct him over to Joella.

"Don't worry, Jo," I whispered, hoping I sounded confident and cheerful. "It will work out. Mom and Dad might even calm down. They may realize that they need us more than we need them."

In a shaky whisper she replied, "They already know that, Carmen." She raised her eyes to meet mine.

"They won't risk losing us both. They depend upon us too much."

"They might be bluffing. Or they may not care how they live." She shrugged. "Do you think they care?"

"They must."

"Then maybe they can learn to take care of themselves. They survived for a lot of years before they had us."

"Mom used to have a job," I said, "but she couldn't work now."

"She always blamed her drinking on us."

"She always blamed her drinking on her arthritis," I contradicted.

"Maybe she blamed us for her arthritis," Joella ventured quietly, sincerely, persistently. "How hard do they have to push you away before you stop coming back to help them?" She lifted her head and looked straight at me with an unexpected amount of poise. "You may have repaid them for giving you life already."

"But life is priceless," I protested.

She countered, "And they have discounted our lives from the days of our births."

"You are so bitter, Jo." I wanted to offer her comfort, but I didn't know how.

She shrugged, almost cheerfully. "Not much lasts in the Trahan household, Carmen. Mom picks everything apart, and Dad allows it all to rust or something just to make sure." Her voice cracked. Cynicism did not come to her naturally.

I placed one of my hands on each of her bony shoulders. She allowed me to touch her and to pull her forward so that we could lean together, my forehead against hers. I felt like I had looked into her grey-blue eyes without actually meeting them. I wasn't that bold. "I love you, Joella. No matter what happens, I want you to know that."

"I already do." She nearly managed a smile.

Then Jo was gone across the sand, standing by Justin, leaning into his arms instead of mine. Her belly was small again, flat as it was when I saw her on Friday. Oleg smiled at me, and the lovers disappeared. Fed up with the way my morning had gone, I wished I could disappear with them. Too much emotion and still no decision. I started to collect my belongings.

"Going back?" Oleg asked. Suddenly his sandals were on his feet and his unused blanket rolled under one arm. "Ready for lunch?" He leaned on his cane while I finished preparing to go. "How was the water?"

"Fantastic," I answered grumpily. My enjoyment of the water had been torn away from me by the battle upon my return. I hastily stuffed the tail end of my towel into my bag and set off to find my way through the low dunes to the wooden walkway about a quarter mile away. It would have been quite the trek for the real Father Oleg. "I forgot about all this fuss for a few minutes. It was good for me to clear my head. I mean, I think that's why I came here. So I could think things through quietly."

He looked surprised. "Your thoughts aren't quiet, sister."

"I guess you'd know, wouldn't you?"

"There's a lot going on in your brain, Carmen."

The sand was painfully hot, and the footing was difficult. It would have been nice if I had outpaced Father Oleg, as I would have in real life, but my subconscious was not as ready as I was to discontinue this quasi-internal dialogue.

"Can I go swimming with you next time? I wouldn't mind taking a break from all this drama myself."

"No," I snapped at him. "And, in case you've changed your mind, you aren't invited to lunch with me anymore. In fact, how long were you planning to stay?"

"That depends upon you. If I stay the weekend, I suppose you'll make me get my own room?"

"You'd better disappear before I go upstairs." There was no way any man, even an imaginary priest, was going to share my bedroom with me. "Nothing personal."

"I'll sleep on a couch in the lobby."

"Works for me." I was tired of him. I wanted to blame him for everything, yet I knew better. This was my fault, or Joella's, or my parents', but it was definitely not his, no matter how much he annoyed me. As we approached the hotel grounds, I tried to be more polite. I held back to talk to him where we would not be witnessed. "What can you tell me about Justin?"

Oleg studied me. When he was analyzing something, I could always see it in his face. All of his features seemed to shrink slightly or his skull grew larger as his big thoughts inflated it. "It's all a guess."

"If he's a normal eighteen year old boy," I insisted.

He raised an eyebrow. "Whatever that is," under his breath. "Okay. Presumably, he's decent. He'll be scared shitless by your parents, his sergeant, and the Taliban." With a shrug, he went on. "He's probably glad to be away and doesn't want to think about what's happening at home without him. He has enough to think about. Probably wants sweet love letters from Joella, and not to hear about any problems she's having, though he must know she has problems at home. Not including her current, uh, predicament. Was that what your folks called it?"

"So what does that mean? How is he likely to react?"

"He'll manage. It won't all seem real to him until he gets home, and by then he'll have grown used to the idea. Pretty much."

"You have connections in the military, don't you? You can get some chaplain to help him? You can't tell me that Justin is the only soldier leaving behind more than a steady girl."

"Hardly."

"So? You will help Joella?"

"You can rely on Father Oleg, Carmen."

I turned inland again, resuming my course to the hotel. I had only gone a step when I felt his hand grab my elbow.

"Don't you think you can just hand her care off to me, even the real me. You cannot do that. I can't be a replacement sister."

"I wouldn't," I began, but then I knew he was correct. I would have loved to pass along this problem.

I left him behind after that. When I gained the walkway, I looked back to see him stumbling through the sand. I didn't look back a second time, but rushed until I was under the awning that covered the last section of the walk. Fans turned above my head, cooling me, cooling my emotions. My heavy tread lightened to a normal walk. My eyes began to adjust to the shade, and I found a certain amount of comfort in the presence of the real strangers around me.

CHAPTER THREE

I leaned against the back wall of the elevator in an imitation of relaxation. I had a healthy salt and sunshine thirst, so I wanted to clean up and get downstairs to the coffee shop before I found a reason to think about anything other than what kind of cold drink I should order with my lunch.

Outside of my room I froze, shocked to hear my mother's voice coming from the other side of the door. I stared at the lock box, trying to shut down the complaining tone of her voice, unwilling to put my key into the slot until it stopped. I was suddenly fearful that I hadn't the energy to silence it. I'm not sure how many minutes I stood paralyzed, holding my key out in front of me. I lost track of the reality around me enough that when I heard a man's voice beside me I jumped. The sharp tones of my mother's voice ended abruptly.

He spoke again. "Miss?" I was struck by the politeness of his intrusion. It was no wonder that my phantom mother had been vanquished. "Do you need help?"

I jumped. "Oh no!" I replied with embarrassment. "No, I'm okay. No, I don't need help." I spoke too quickly, agitated and sounding as if I might be beyond help. With what I'm sure was a silly smile, I rushed to add, subconsciously truthful, "It's just my imagination going wild." I inserted my keycard in the door, got a green light, and pushed it open. "Yep. Everything's okay." I nodded to reassure him, but I needed to be convinced far more than he did, so I added a temperate, "Thanks."

"Of course," he responded with a courteous nod, and he continued on further down the hall.

Now that I was alone, I felt grateful for his attention and the fact that I had spoken to another real person.

I threw some water on my face, tidied my hair, and changed into my dry clothing, shorts and a t-shirt, before hurrying back to the outer world where real people could protect me. Within moments I entered the glossy, bright coffee shop on the second floor, the hotel's main eatery for breakfast and lunch. It was busy but large enough to handle the crowd, with seats indoors and out on one of the hotel's many terraces.

I asked to be seated inside. I was shown to a table for two along the lemon yellow banquette, where I sat looking out into the dining room. The waitress promptly brought me a glass of water and asked if I had any questions about the menu I'd just opened. Alert to my surroundings now, I turned my attention to its plastic coated pages. There were too many choices, so I selected one of the first things I saw. The waitress returned when I laid my folded menu on the table.

"Can I get a grilled cheese and tomato sandwich? Only I'd like it toasted instead of grilled." Then I paused, still debating my drink order. I was more interested in the drink than the food. Though I was craving lemonade, I decided against the unnecessary calories and requested a diet cola.

I watched the waitress amble toward the kitchen to place my order. She noted the status of her tables with a quick, efficient glance. She looked like a youthful grandmother, kind and active, and it occurred to me that she could probably help me sort through my conundrum better than all the imaginary people I could create in my head.

Once she was around the corner, I pulled a steno pad and a pencil out of my handbag. I would make a list of the various reasons why and why not to help my sister. I hoped this logical approach would help me to analyze the situation objectively. The first idea I had involved other family members, particularly my Aunt Chris, my mother's youngest sister, only about fifty years old like the waitress. Before her family moved to Charleston, she had gone out of her way to include us. I wondered how my extended family would react to Joella's news.

I saw Aunt Chris's face on the blank page. "Joella can live with us, Carmen. You don't have to take all of this on yourself. Everyone in the family will help. We don't hold it against you girls that your mom and dad are selfish idiots." This was the kind of advice I could use, though that last comment was a reminder that this statement had not really come from my aunt's lips. She may have thought such things, but she would never say it out loud in front of me.

I blinked. She was gone, but another distraction appeared. A quiet cough made me look up to see a smiling, dark haired man watching me. "Hello?" I said.

"Forgive me for interrupting, Miss. Are you doing better now?"

My eyes widened as I realized with speechless embarrassment that he was the man from the hall. I hadn't dared to look at him during our first meeting.

"May I join you?"

I continued to stare rudely at him. I made some kind of unintelligible sound and blinked at him again. He didn't disappear the way my aunt had. He was real, but that was not his only appeal. Some unusual instinct told me that it was safe for me to chat with him. His geeky chivalry was natural, but he was too modernly polite to intrude into private matters.

"Sure," I said after a long enough time for his face to redden.

"Thank you." He pulled out the chair opposite mine, and before he finished scooting it in again, the waitress brought him a menu. He opened it, but kept his eyes on me.

I cringed, and he dropped his eyes to the page. "Have you ordered already? I guess she'll want mine too, so she can serve us together." He tilted the menu toward himself to talk to me over it. "It seems kind of rude to interrupt you and then ignore you."

"Under the circumstances…"

"True." His eyes were on the menu again, and I started to breathe more easily. Something about him seemed familiar, beyond my having encountered him in the hall before. When he said, "My name is Dennis," I could have finished the sentence. "And I feel like I should know yours. Karen? Carolyn? You're from Eastmont?"

My eyes narrowed, trying to figure out the situation. "It's Carmen."

"Ah! Church," he said brightly.

"What?" I looked at him again, squinting to place him in a different setting. "You go to Holy Mercy?"

"I used to." He folded his menu and set it on the corner of the table. "I live in another parish now, but my family, mostly, still goes there."

I didn't say anything.

"So, are your parents opera buffs? Do you have a little Spanish in you?"

"No," I replied. Then I realized he was talking about my name so I tried to hold up my end of our first awkward conversation. "I don't know how they picked my name. I always had this weird idea that my dad stole a Karmann Ghia once." I laughed to make him think I was joking.

"You don't see many of those anymore, so I guess it would be worth a little bragging," he replied, amused. "I'm surprised they never told you. Parents are usually so proud of the names they choose. And yours is pretty. My parents told me they had names pinned to a cork board, and they threw darts at it." He chuckled at his own story.

"I never thought to ask," I replied. I didn't want to understand the way my parents thought.

The waitress came to take his order. He ordered at least double the amount of food I had. After she left, he whispered across the table, "I'm saving room for dessert. I promised myself I'd visit Cliff's Creamery every day while I'm here." I smiled at his enthusiasm. Perhaps he always enjoyed life. How enviable.

"So this is a small meal?" I asked in a conspiratorial whisper.

"Well, you know how hungry you get when you swim," he explained. "The ocean was glorious this morning. Did you get to swim yet?"

"Yes. It was very nice. It was gentler than I expected."

"The beach here is partly protected by Crimson Island. It's a barrier island," he added seeing that I didn't know what he was talking about. "South of here. Forms the outside of Lofton's harbor." He continued talking about ocean currents, and I nodded, appreciating his apparent level of knowledge, but not understanding anything beyond the fact that the outer island protected the inner shore. After a while he must have sensed that I had nothing to contribute, so he changed the subject. I almost didn't notice because I had just been listening to his pleasant voice without attending to the words. "When did you get here, Carmen?"

"About two o'clock this morning."

"I hope someone else was driving so you could sleep."

"Y'I was on the bus."

"I took Friday off, and I drove down the coast and did a little exploring. I want to do some more of that during the week, or at the least on my way back home," he told me.

We continued to converse, and it grew easier, during our meal, which was delivered maybe five minutes after his order was taken. He called me a nibbler, and I ended up eating my whole sandwich, my appetite whetted by his.

"You want to go with me for ice cream, Carmen? It'll be too hot to use the beach for a while."

Confused, I reacted by laughing, which was probably rather unkind. I think he'd just asked me for a date, and I wasn't sure what to do. I liked talking to him, but I didn't know where to set my boundaries. I had to wonder if I was using him to escape the isolation I had planned for this weekend the way I had earlier with my personal priest.

"Have I embarrassed you? I'm sorry."

I blushed, and though I still wasn't sure if it was alright, I told him it was.

"I never do know quite how to go from total stranger to friendly acquaintance. Especially when I meet someone all on my own, like this. It's much less intimidating when someone introduces you or you work at the same place or something." He stopped to evaluate my fight or flight status. "Well, I mean, I just loved the idea of your imagination going wild and keeping you out of your room." He tried to say it lightly, but didn't quite succeed. "You writing a story?"

"Me? Oh, no. I'm just making lists." I closed my note pad, which was still on the table under my left elbow, and popped it into my handbag. I had written nothing on it.

"I won't ask, but I hope you're making a list of the things you want to do while you're here."

"I don't need a list for that," I replied, settling down again. "All I want to do is go to the beach and relax."

"How long are you staying here?"

"I'm going home tomorrow. I have to be back at work on Tuesday."

"What do you do?"

"I'm a hairstylist."

"Cool," he said so naturally that I believed him.

"I like it."

"I imagine it's a steady business. People always need haircuts."

"Yeah," I agreed. "I'm in a good shop, and I'm starting to build a clientele. I've been licensed for a little over a year now."

"What do you have to do to get a license? Beauty school?"

"And then an apprenticeship." I nodded. "What about you?"

"I'm a mechanical engineer." That bright smile again. No wonder he could explain ocean currents.

"Impressive."

"Not really," he laughed. "But it's fun. On a good day, I get dirty and play with machines."

"I usually get wet," I offered.

He lifted one hand. "High five," and we slapped. His hand was damp from the condensation on his glass. Or nervous sweat. "You still want ice cream?"

I laughed again. "I never said I did."

"Come on, now. It's better than any you can get at home."

"Probably."

"When was the last time you had fresh ice cream?"

I shrugged.

"That settles it. You need this. You've got to come."

"Need? Ice cream is hardly a necessity," I protested.

He straightened his posture, rejecting my argument. "Do I need to remind you that it will be too hot to be on the beach for the next couple of hours?"

I smiled at last. "No, you don't need to remind me."

"Good. Let's go."

He guided me out of the hotel to the street, making sure that I didn't slip away on some more serious mission. He restarted our conversation. "Do you still live in Strickland?"

"I'm in Azalea Grove now."

"Where did you grow up? My folks live off Collier Spring Road."

"Gifford Street."

"I still go to the church sometimes, when Mom invites me for breakfast. Maybe I'll see y'around sometime. It's cool that we have a connection in the real world." He didn't say anything until we were across the next street.

"Where do you live now?"

"Princeton, near the docks. I ride my bike to work. Do you work in Azalea Grove?"

"No. My shop's on Doyle Row. It's called Georges. It's way too expensive to live near there."

"Yah," he agreed. "But I hope your customers can afford it."

I smiled. "Most of them. Although do you remember Father Oleg? He comes to me for haircuts." Why did I mention him?

"Awesome." Then he asked in a skeptical tone, "So you don't think ice cream is necessary?"

"It's a special treat," I replied.

"I have a feeling that you don't let yourself have special treats very often." He looked at me sidelong. "Especially if they involve food."

I couldn't think of a reply, and we walked in silence. The sidewalks radiated white heat. There hadn't been a stir of breeze until we were inland two or three blocks and uphill enough to see between the tall hotels and over the dunes to the water. We entered the older commercial area where I had wandered with the other children on my earlier visit. This part of town had lots of green spaces, parks with trees and lawns. The cliffs provided a backdrop to everything. I'd never been in a place where so much of the sky was blocked; surprisingly, it made me feel safe, like I was in a hiding place. I thought that I might be happier sleeping in one of these parks than in my elegant room in the Neptune Hotel.

We got into the line at Cliff's Creamery. Once I got close enough to see the choices available I could see why the line was so long. There must have been thirty different flavors of ice cream and sherbet, and beyond that, choices of cones, syrups, crushed candies, and sodas.

"Get whatever you want, Carmen," Dennis said, speed reading the list of selections.

"There are too many choices," I said quietly.

"Yeah," he agreed. "I keep meaning to try something exotic, but I always end up just getting a cone."

"That's what I want."

"Pick a flavor yet?" We were already nearing the cash register.

"Strawberry."

He raised an eyebrow. "That's not terribly daring."

How *did* he know about *that*? "Sorry. It's my favorite."

"You can't go wrong then." He nodded. "How many scoops?"

"One! Please remember, I just ate a big lunch."

"You nibbled at your lunch. You probably left half of it on your plate," he replied.

After we walked away from the shop, licking the sides of the enormous scoops, trying to catch the drips before they fell to our fingers or fronts, I said, "This is the best ice cream I've ever had."

He smiled. "Mine's good too." He bit into a lump of his double chocolate chunk whatever—I think there were walnuts and marshmallows in it too—with his lips. "Let's get into the shade before we lose this race."

Where we sat, under a tree, we picked up some of the wind off the ocean. "So, Carmen," he began. "You seem preoccupied. Anything you want to talk about?" He was dangerously intuitive.

"What?" My head popped up. "No. I'm fine."

"You sure? I've found that sometimes it's easier to talk to a stranger. I think I still qualify as one of those."

"Thanks, but no, Dennis." I tried to laugh.

He could see that I was skimming dishonesty. He was also insecure about asking me about it. "I respect your privacy." Then he changed the subject. "Are you planning to go back to the beach this afternoon?"

"I think so."

"Would you like to hang out, or shall I go to the pool?"

I was enjoying his company, but I didn't feel ready to spend the whole afternoon with him. And he was distracting me from my mission.

"Tell you what, Carmen," he said, answering his own question before I figured out how to reject him. "You go to the beach. I'll use the pool. I want to swim laps." He nodded his head, showing his earnestness. "And, perhaps I could take you to supper tonight?"

"Really?" I exclaimed without thinking. I was reacting to his first statement, that he wanted to separate for the afternoon, but I quickly realized that he thought I had enthusiastically accepted his dinner invitation. Luckily, I was not averse to having dinner with him. "I mean, that sounds nice," I covered quietly.

He smiled. He looked very happy. "I'll knock around seven?"

"Okay." As I fought the urge to smile, I realized that I was looking forward to seeing him again later.

"We'll go someplace casual. Away from the hotel."

I looked around our shady green place. "These parks are really nice."

"It's like an oasis. The sun doesn't scorch so much." We were nearly done with the part of the ice cream that hadn't dripped down our wrists to the grass. Luckily we had been supplied with large paper napkins and moist towelettes. Still we both held our cones out away from our clothes. "Guess we should have gotten dishes."

"Mmm."

He noticed me looking at the face of the cliff, my head tilting to find the line at the top where the sky reappeared. "In a few hours, it will all be shaded here."

"Really?" I blinked. "Yes, I suppose it must be very pleasant then." I was starting to return to my shell to save my sociability for the evening. When he asked if he could walk me back to the hotel, I accepted. I tried to seem easygoing, like it was an everyday thing to walk about with a nice man. We didn't say much on our way back to the hotel. Just inside the revolving doors, he reminded me to be ready at seven o'clock, and then he went to find a newspaper.

I went through the lobby to the elevator. Though I wasn't looking around, I still caught sight of Father Oleg, sprawled on one of the sofas, relaxing with his eyes closed. I half-hoped that he had gone to rest for the night, but I knew better than to believe he would leave me alone for that long a time.

CHAPTER FOUR

My mind ambushed me again when I re-entered my hotel room and found Joella asleep on my bed. While I was out flirting and overeating, she had collapsed from sheer exhaustion. I hadn't even noticed she was tired when I saw her on Friday, but of course she must have been. She was probably drained.

I had been too busy thinking about how everything was going to affect me to consider her needs.

On Friday afternoon, Joella had slunk into the salon as I was rolling the last few rods into Tara Blake's hair for a permanent. I signaled for my sister to sit while she waited for me, one hand held in the air with the five fingers splayed to signify five minutes. She squirmed in the chair while she tried to look at a magazine. I finished rolling Mrs. Blake's hair and then squirted on the first dose of chemicals with pursed lips.

"Something wrong, Carmen?" Mrs. Blake asked.

"My little sister just came in, and she looks upset."

She nodded. "Is that her? Fanning herself with the magazine? She looks a lot like you."

"Thank you," I said. I thought that Joella was a very pretty girl. She didn't need to watch her weight like I did. A few minutes later, as I neared her, Joella tilted her head toward the door, and we went outside. She directed me down the sidewalk in front of the shops and around the corner at the end of the row of buildings. This was the place the smokers went for their breaks. One could watch the storefronts from there, and I stood where I could watch for my next client.

"What's the matter, Jo?"

She looked ready to choke, but she spoke clearly. "I'm pregnant," she said, and then she burst into tears.

I stared at her, shocked immobile, unable to speak or move. Only once I saw my next customer walking up to the shop's door over Jo's shoulder did I begin to move again. She put her hands on my forearms to support me, fearing that I might keel over because I had forgotten to breathe. When I took a step backward, she stepped forward, not allowing a gap to form between us. I still said nothing, but watched her tear-streaked face, red enough to camouflage her freckles, from the distance of her arm's length. She lifted her head and met my eyes. She seemed strong, defiant even, showing a determined streak I had rarely had the opportunity to witness. I looked away, feeling as if I had lost a test of wills, though there was no reason for one to have taken place between us.

I thought that I should take the lead since she had come to me, her older sister, for help and advice. "Jo." I tried to sound calm. "Jo, are you sure?"

She nodded. Then she put her hand in her pocket and pulled out the test strip from her home pregnancy test. She had to tell me what it was, and I looked at it with no idea how to interpret it. "This showed a positive," she explained in a clinical tone. "They never have false positives." When I just continued looking at her and it, my mouth probably hanging open, she continued. "You've never taken one?"

"No. I've never had a reason to suspect I was pregnant."

"Oh." She sounded disappointed. Perhaps she was hoping I had already worked my way through some of the issues she was now facing. Maybe she just wanted someone to understand what she was going through. Well, I couldn't, and I didn't catch on soon enough that I should have pretended I did.

"Do you know how far along you are, Jo?"

"At least two months."

"Okay. Well, you're not too far along yet."

"What are you thinking?" she asked, recoiling. She must have been afraid I was going to suggest she get an abortion.

"Just that I wanted to know when the baby might come, and how long you had before you had to tell Mom and Dad. There's time to make a plan."

"Some time, yes." She relaxed slightly. "Mom will have an inkling soon enough though. I don't have long."

"The father is this Justin I've been hearing about, right?"

Looking offended, she did not reply.

"I'm sorry. I mean, he's gone now, right?"

"Yes."

"Do you know how he might feel about this?"

"About as scared as I am."

"Jo, I've got to go back to work. Wait for me. I promise I'll talk to you about this more."

"Okay." She hung her head.

"You have something to do while you wait? Homework?"

"Did it already."

"Should have brought it and come earlier. I'm only going to get busier now as it gets later." I had a chart full of cuts, curls, and colors.

"I guess I should have come yesterday."

"We'd've had more time." With that, I went inside again and greeted my next client. She stayed outside, leaning against the stonework under the plate glass window, facing the street, small and solitary.

Forty-five minutes later, I had a chance to speak with her at greater length. She was more talkative, I guess having already made her announcement, she was ready to think and feel other things. At times her words were so quick I had trouble keeping up with my listening, but I got the important parts. "Mom's going to kill me," she said rapidly. "Can I move in with you? Will you help me, Carmen?"

I was frozen, a jumble of words tangled up in my voice box nearly choking me. Nothing came out. I could breathe; I just couldn't speak. That my mother's reaction might be violent was no surprise, but my sister's wanting to shelter with me was. At least *I* wasn't prepared to answer her.

Joella stared into my face, transfixed with worry, possibly for me, probably for her. "I know it's a lot to ask. And I don't have a lot to offer you in return, especially in the beginning. I promise I'll help as much as I can with rent and everything once I start working. I'll do all that I can. And hopefully when Justin comes home, he'll...help."

At last a subject I dared approach. "What about him, Jo? How do you think he'll handle this news?"

Her eyes filled again, and her voice shook. "We love each other, Carmen."

"Okay, that's good, but you're both so young."

She didn't let me finish. "That doesn't really matter, does it? We've not had the chance to learn much yet, but we've got everything before us. Isn't that mostly a good thing? Look at our parents, Carmen. They were over forty when they had us, and we both know what a splendid job they did raising us." The bitterness in her voice showed on her face as well.

"We've turned out well, mostly," I said.

"Miraculously."

"Do you really hate them, Joella? I know things could have been better, but with their problems it's understandable that they couldn't always cope with raising us. Can't you forgive them? Don't you love them anyway?"

"I do hate them, Carmen, and I love them too, but I don't like them and I won't forgive them. Their problems are of their own making."

"So are yours," I said calmly. Yet for a moment I envied her certainty. Once I had longed to be out from under their roof, but it was long ago, and the reasons for my hurry to go seemed selfish now. I don't think I ever felt as wronged as Joella did. I pitied my parents. They were in their sixties. They had no friends and had lost touch with most of their family members. They had no one but us, and though that was their own fault, it was still pathetic.

My father had spent his life as a manual laborer, and though he seemed healthy and strong, his body was starting to show serious signs of wear. His knees and back pained him. I'd seen him struggle to rise from a chair. He was not the kind of man who would be inspired to build a new set of skills for his life after he could no longer do the kind of work he had always done.

My mother's arthritis had led to inactivity and weight gain, and more recently the excess weight had brought on diabetes. Movement was painful, and she had used pain medication since I was small. Before I was born she had worked at a bakery, and she even had a small pension for her retirement years from this job, but she could never go back to doing that kind of work again, nor even, though her mind was sharp, could she have kept up the pace at any kind of work place.

"Do you hate me too, Joella?" I asked, dreading the answer.

"Oh dear, Carmen. No," she said, putting a consolatory hand on my arm, "I love you, and I like you, and I admire you very much."

"Would you hate me if I didn't take you in?"

She looked confused. I'm sure she wanted to say, "And why wouldn't you?" but instead she just said, "No. I wouldn't hate you." She tried to swallow her disappointment, and mostly succeeded in convincing me that she was in control of her emotions. "I might even come to understand it. I know you feel bound to them, and so do I, to a point. And I suppose I shouldn't force you to choose between us. I don't know how to be fair to you, Carmen."

I felt anger rising, but managed to restrain it.

"I know that I'm asking something huge of you."

"Yes, Joella, you are asking a terrible lot of me. I don't know that we could actually live in my room together, especially if the baby lives with you."

"I will keep the baby," she stated quickly. Her hand went to her belly. "This child was made in love, Carmen. I won't be parted from Justin's child."

"Justin might feel differently." My tone was cold.

"I'll manage, then, on my own somehow."

"With my help?"

"Well, yes." She hung her head. "For a while."

"Right now, I'm worried about getting this past our folks."

"Alright," she said more calmly. "I'll admit that is the first hurdle. I cannot stay with them. You know that. I have to leave. I can't allow them a chance to harm my baby."

"And this is all about you, isn't it, Jo?"

"What?"

"It's all about what you want. You want to move out. You want to keep the baby. You're setting all the terms," I accused her, raising my voice.

"Okay, Carmen. You're right. I'm demanding and selfish. I feel that I need to be." She was working to keep her cool. "I'm preoccupied with my future and that of my child. I have to learn how to protect this thing inside of me, though it doesn't feel real to me yet."

"It's real enough that you've come looking for help."

"I know it is real." Her voice was steadier when she spoke again. "I want you to understand, Carmen, that I've discovered love, and I'm not planning to ever do without it again." She leaned her shoulder against the wall and took a few deep breaths, and I didn't interrupt. "I love Justin, and whether we have a future together or not, I will always be grateful to him. And to his family for accepting me just because I was important to him. That's all it took. It wasn't difficult."

"Jo." I almost protested, but I couldn't argue. I didn't know; I wasn't certain that she was wrong.

"I want my child to grow up surrounded by love." She bowed her head slightly. "I know you think we are responsible for Mom and Dad. I'm not going to say that we don't owe them something. I didn't intend to shove another wedge into our family. I'm afraid that I am anyway, and that I am forcing you to choose between them and me forever. I'm sorry. I know you want to stay on good terms with them. But I'd rather go through this with you than anyone else. You're my big sister."

Maybe she did admire me. She clearly knew my dread, my very thoughts. She knew as well as I did that there was no way for us to stick together over this without abandoning our folks. They had volatile temperaments, and they always brought out the worst in each other. They were both incredibly stubborn. To my knowledge they had never let go of a grudge in their lives, and they saw no reason why they ever should. But I still I owed them my loyalty.

"Who knows?" she said without enthusiasm. "Maybe they will shock us both and accept the situation with grace." She had an odd smile on her face that irritated me.

"Oh, yes. That's very realistic, Jo," I replied harshly, my sympathy evaporating. "Were you already pregnant when they grounded you and forbade your seeing Justin again?" Something snapped, and I turned on her. Though I knew she was very young and impressionable, I really could not understand how she could have risked her future this way. I would never have let a boy seduce me. Why should she? She wasn't stupid. Why would she be so foolish?

"I don't think so," she replied quietly.

"So you still found opportunities?" I stepped into the space that divided us, cornering her.

"Of course," she said as if this was the most obvious thing anyone had ever put into words. "After getting in so much trouble just for falling asleep on his parents' sofa, there wasn't much point in following their rules, was there?"

"Did you get pregnant on purpose?" It was more of an accusation than a question. "Did Justin know what he was doing?"

"No, I didn't get pregnant on purpose," she answered impatiently. She pushed off the wall to stand upright again. "It was that Justin was leaving, and us thinking about how we'd be apart for, like, probably at least a year. We needed to touch each other. I wanted so much to be close to him."

"Sounds like you were so angry with Mom and Dad for grounding you that you decided to get even by spreading your legs for that boy anytime you got ten seconds alone?"

"No! That's not at all the way it was," she cried out in self-defense. "I was happy when I was with Justin. I did what I did with him because I love him. It had nothing to do with Mom and Dad treating me unfairly."

"Didn't they forbid you seeing him? You ignored their rules."

"So what if I did? They treat me like dirt even when I do everything they want me to."

My voice was as harsh as her words. I sounded like our mother, but at the time it didn't bother me. "It sounds like they should have been stricter with you. Not just laying down rules, but enforcing them too."

"Well, thank God they can't enforce all of their rules. Most of their rules are stupid, and you know it." As abrasive as I was, she kept her poise. She argued without yelling. "If they were any harder on me, I'd have run off long ago."

"And asked for my help?"

"Maybe."

I made an excuse to break off the conversation. "I've got a customer coming in again, Jo. I don't know what I can do to help you." I was weary. My behavior was scaring me, and I was growing frustrated with my inability to remain civil. I really didn't want to alienate her. "My place isn't big enough for you and me and a baby. I don't know if I can afford a bigger place yet. I don't have much to spare."

She passed over my practical objections, and pled the emotional reasons for me to take her in. "They treat me like shit, Carmen, and they didn't treat you any better even though you were more obedient. Do I need to remind you how you lied and sneaked around to get out of the house the very first instant you could get out of the door?" It came out like an accusation. "I'm sick of taking it from them."

I walked around her from where I stood farther back in the alley than I had known myself to be on my way inside to take care of my client, forcing myself to center my attention on my work. Bad news couldn't affect my scissor and comb control. I could see Joella through the plate glass, pouting and looking ever so young. And terrified. Finally, my heart was touched. I didn't want to hurt her, but I couldn't see how she could ever be reconciled with our parents. No matter how many years passed, they would hold this rebellion against her.

Then and there I should have sent her home to my place where she could have rested and waited for me. I could have let her news sink in instead of reacting through shock. We could have had slow hours to talk and reconnect, to better understand each other and our positions. But I didn't have the wherewithal to offer her a dignified way through this first meeting. All I could think about was getting away from her problems, and now I'd been here in Lofton Beach for something like fifteen hours and I'd made no progress at all. Poor Joella. She really had been left stranded.

I suppose that this is the way it usually is with unplanned pregnancies. If they were convenient or delightful, they would be called "surprise blessings" or something that sounded positive. "Unplanned" implies that something went wrong. Her face, her whole manner supported this interpretation.

"I don't know what I can do, Jo. I can't promise you anything," I said the next time we spoke, about twenty minutes later. "Not yet. I've got to think about things. I'm still worried about Mom and Dad."

She understood this better than I expected. "They know better than to rely on me." She didn't say much after that. I thought we had talked it through as well as we could when the only thing conclusive was the result shown on that test strip of hers. She promised that she would go home before our folks grew suspicious. I told her not to try to talk to me this weekend. I was already forming an escape plan. When I heard the manicurist discussing a beach trip with one of her clients, I decided that I would be on the bus to Lofton Beach as soon as I left work the following night. I packed my bag on Friday evening and logged onto Robert's internet during a break on Saturday to make reservations.

And now I was here: away. Away was nice. I could think about all of this from a distance and I could escape it in weak moments. I sincerely wanted to do the right thing with the right consequences, but part of me felt like blowing everything the way Joella may already have done.

She had this romantic notion about keeping the baby and Justin coming home from the War on Terror ready to care for them both. She harbored this dream of everything turning out right, yet it was deeply buried beneath her practical knowledge that our parents would at the very best treat her as a second rate person for the rest of her life.

I thought that it was too soon for Joella to decide if she would keep her baby. As her pregnancy ran its course, she needed to investigate her options. I knew that she thought it would be selfish and wrong for her to place the baby for adoption if there was any hope that she and Justin would stay together, which was possible. They were in love. He probably possessed some of the decency she claimed he had. He had been kind enough to ask nothing of Joella when he left, unless one considers the seed he left behind. Even that I could almost understand. If I were a boy potentially heading into combat, I wouldn't worry about birth control either. I probably wouldn't even worry about diseases. I made a mental note to remind Joella that she should be tested for more than pregnancy when she saw the doctor, but I never bothered to write it down, because I imagined that it was something the doctor would think of on her own.

CHAPTER FIVE

I let Joella sleep. We didn't need to have another conversation until we could be together to have a real one. It made me feel better to think that she was resting. Besides I wanted to get back out on the beach. I was eager to get into the water again. My desire for activity came more from energy than anxiety now, perhaps from meeting Dennis. It occurred to me that I might have been missing more than I realized by avoiding masculine society.

On my earlier venture to the shore, I had learned that the hotels provided towels as well as umbrellas and chairs out on the open beach, so I just threw my magazine into my bag along with my water bottle, dumped and refilled from the tap. I passed the pool yard without looking through the fence; Dennis was probably there already. As fast as I got ready to go out again, there wasn't a chance it could compare to a man's speed in preparing for a sporting activity. I was still grateful to him for letting me have the beach to myself.

Father Oleg was not so generous. He was sunning himself on a deckchair at the side of the wooden walk, watching for me. He rose when I came near. "Have a nice lunch?" he asked as a greeting, and he fell in hobbling at my side.

My only response was a brief glare.

"What did I do?" he asked, looking wounded, and when I didn't answer, which I mainly didn't do because I wasn't quite sure why he deserved this bit of bad attitude from me, he went on. "Did you have a good time with your new friend? Are you planning to sleep with him?"

"Oh, for Heaven's sake!" I cried out loudly and impatiently. "When did my conscience become so annoying?" Then I dropped my gaze to my feet, embarrassed that I had said this aloud in the presence of other people. I was too slow to avoid meeting the amusement on the faces of my witnesses, an elderly couple walking arm-in-arm toward me.

Oleg answered without hesitation, ignoring them as he could with his invisibility. "I suppose when you picked an annoying priest to come along for these little internal chats."

"Oleg Fuentes isn't *this* annoying," I thought.

"He's never had much reason to pester you."

I had to agree, but I didn't admit it. I just changed the subject. "Are you going to keep following me around?"

"I've never been one to turn down such a friendly invitation."

"My, you must have a feeble social life."

He shrugged. He could have compared mine to his, but he spared me that. "The good father may not have pestered you, but you've got a pretty good take on his personality. He's annoyed plenty of people in his time."

"I think I'll talk to my aunt about helping Joella after I get back," I stated bluntly.

"That's a good idea. Keep yourself in the will. Aunt Chris wouldn't miss the share your folks weren't planning to leave her."

"That is not what this is about," I protested. We came over the last bridge to the expanse of flat, pale sand. The boardwalk continued until we were much closer to the water, where it joined another that ran parallel to the shore.

"It must figure in somewhere, Carmen, or I wouldn't have said it. Remember, I am only a voice for your own thoughts."

"And how could I forget?" I mumbled back. "But my folks don't have anything, and I doubt they have bothered to write wills. I'll probably have to pay for their funerals and clear up some debts with my own money."

"So does talking to your aunt count as helping Joella?" When I didn't answer, he changed the subject again. "Beach looks great."

"Yeah. I'm going to swim and read and ignore you for a while."

He parked his free hand on his hip and looked at me with a bit of a scowl. "Go ahead and try. You are having a rough time denying your attraction."

"My attraction? To what? To you?" I sputtered, laughing awkwardly. I may have seemed guilty as charged, but he was wrong. "Not in the least."

"Now you're awake." He smiled, enjoying this baiting game.

"Look, if I said what I want to say to you," I hissed between my teeth, "I'd be arrested or committed or something."

"You can say whatever you want into the pages of your periodical," he suggested.

I almost said he knew me too well, but then—hello—he was me, so to speak. I found a vacant umbrella and spread a fresh towel on one of the wooden lounge chairs. Oleg sat on the edge of the other one, leaning forward with his elbows on his knees and his eyes fixed on the sand at his feet. He picked up his cane and ran the tip of it across the sand. He left no mark.

"What are you doing?" I asked.

"Doodling. Sort of. I'm not terribly artistic." He glanced up at my face, which must have carried a sour expression. "What's eating at you now? You had a good time at lunch. I'd have thought that the prospect of a new boyfriend would raise your spirits, but you're even crabbier than you were this morning."

"I ate too much," I grumbled.

"Which you should have enjoyed." He continued dragging his cane across the sand, but he was just swinging it back and forth like a malfunctioning windshield wiper. "That's not what's bothering you."

"Well, you know best."

"Could be." He dropped his cane and looked up. "You're afraid you're turning into your mother."

That was too close. I changed the subject. "What would you have done if one of your sisters got pregnant like Joella?"

"Become an uncle, I guess," he replied smugly.

I was tempted to slap him until I remembered he wasn't really there. Maybe *I was* turning into my mother. "Please God, no," I whispered inside my brain. To him I said, "It's more complicated than that."

"Maybe not." He shrugged. "My sister would have talked to my parents, and I wouldn't have had a lot to do with it."

"Would they have let her do what she wanted? Would they have punished her?"

"If she was Joella's age they would have probably helped her decide how *she* wanted to handle things. I'm sure they would have done their best to stay far enough out of it that she wouldn't hold anything against them down the line. They would also try to keep their disappointment hidden, especially around the baby."

"Why especially around the baby?"

He straightened, preparing to give me a lecture. "Because the baby, the child must grow up feeling loved and wanted. Children should always be treated with love. If the family can't welcome the child, what kind of home will they provide? Before that baby is born, you have to accept it as a thinking, feeling, independent person." He watched me carefully as he spoke.

How was it that my own imagination could voice such unfamiliar thoughts? "As a person?" I mumbled.

"It will be a person soon enough, God willing."

"It will make her life so much harder. And mine too, even if I don't help her."

"Yes. Children require a lot of attention, but they rarely ruin people's lives. You adjust. The difficulties will ease; Joella will mature; Justin may become involved in a good way; and you'll love that niece or nephew so much, you'll not feel the burden as heavily as you think you will now."

"Will I?"

"Probably."

"I don't have enough space in my apartment for two people and a baby."

"Two adults and a child," he corrected me.

"And I can't afford a bigger one, especially because I'll have to spend more money on food and all."

"Well, you can't let them stay with your folks. It wouldn't be safe. No matter what you decide, that is not an option."

"Would I be letting her down if she lived with someone else, like our aunt?"

"If it's a happy arrangement, why would you think you were letting her down?"

He put his feet up and leaned back into his lounge chair, studying the ocean through the sunglasses which had just appeared on his somewhat crooked nose. I'd have to ask him sometime, when I was really with him, how it had been broken. I suspected it was during a bar fight before his leg was crushed. The breeze even blew his brown hair. I thought that I should be less comfortable than I was about accepting the products of my imagination. Instead I relaxed. He was quiet for a time, and I nearly forgot he was there until he asked, "So where's that dude you went off with earlier?"

"He was going to the pool."

"Didn't he like you? I could tell you liked him."

"He liked me. We're having dinner together tonight."

"*Are* you going to sleep with him, then?"

"Good God! Can't you act like a priest for one minute?"

"I'm the priest you like, remember?"

"Well." I thought that might no longer be true. "Just because I like a man, doesn't mean that I should glue myself to his side."

"So shouldn't you be painting your nails or something? Primping for your date."

"Painting my—" I blustered. "For Pete's sake!"

"Is his name Pete?"

"No, it's Dennis."

"Is he a nerd? Dennis is a nerd name."

I shrugged. "He's a little nerdy," I admitted. "But he's cute, and I had fun with him."

"So you won't be shagging him tonight," he announced.

I snapped back, "I have no intention of, did you say shagging?"

He laughed, and then made another observation. "Nerds tend to get good paychecks."

"You are awfully obsessed with money, Father," I observed.

"I am not," he protested.

"I've always wondered: do priests and nuns get paid? How does it work?"

"If you don't know, how should I? You'll have to ask Oleg Fuentes *incarnate*."

"How very clerical of you to worm that expression into casual conversation."

"You're a clever girl."

"I wish." I felt the weight of my future niece or nephew again. "If I were clever, I might have already figured out how to handle this."

Oleg reached over to take my hand. "Start by being honest, Carmen."

I glowered at him. "What the hell is that supposed to mean?" I snapped back, jerking my hand away. "You think I can lie to myself? That's nuts!"

"This whole thing is nuts, Carmen," he returned. "If you were being honest with yourself, you wouldn't be using this clever, little conversation method to keep yourself distracted from some of the things that might impact your decisions about helping your sister. If you were being honest, wouldn't you be working this out alone, or with your sister, or with the real me, or with that waitress?"

"You think I'm not being fair about this? I'm only considering that my poor little sister is probably better able to take care of herself and her baby than my parents will be to take care of themselves in a few years. I'm trying not to put too much weight on the fact that I like her better than I like them. That's not supposed to matter in families. We aren't supposed to play favorites. Besides my parents gave us everything. We owe them everything in return."

"That's what your parents taught you, but is that the way they treated you? Didn't they always put their own needs ahead of yours, even if that need was liquor? Your dad's a passive aggressive drunk, and your mother can barely function for two hours straight."

"That doesn't matter."

"Look, we all know you're better than they are…"

I didn't notice that I had risen until I realized I was standing, staring down at him. "What are you getting at, Oleg? What are you accusing me of now?"

"Me? I just like you better than I like your parents. I hope to continue feeling that way. If you want to make a martyr of yourself, then you should make damn sure that it's for a good cause. That's all I'm saying. There's plenty of martyrs in Hell, and intentions don't mean everything."

"How do you know? Been visiting recently?"

"You bet. I want to make sure I get a spot close to the fire." He smiled. "I'd hate to end up spending eternity in the icy part."

I didn't answer aloud. I didn't actually need to speak at all, of course. He read my thoughts, and responded to them the same as if I had spoken.

"So, Joella thinks they never wanted her, and you're worried that might be the case with you too. You never rebelled, but you've stayed out of their way. You were their only child for seven years—and maybe they wanted to have children when they had you. Maybe they thought they could handle children. Maybe they would have managed fine if they had only had you, one child instead of two. But you've been gone, and so she's been an only child for the last seven years. You planned for yourself, but wouldn't they have kept on making demands on you as long as you were under their control? Why don't you tell them where you live? Where you work? All they have is a telephone number, and you screen your calls. You practically raised Joella. They were always telling you to do more around the house and complaining about the cost of everything from your clothes to feeding you?"

"I am not holding a grudge," I declared.

"Really?" he smiled, baiting me again.

"That is not what this is about."

"Fair enough." He stopped and watched me. "So what is Joella planning to do after she graduates?"

"Get a job, I guess." I was exhausted.

"She wants to go to college," he told me. "She wants to be a teacher."

I nodded slowly, remembering. "She's always wanted to, but I've never figured out how she planned to make it happen." With a baby, it would really be impossible. "She isn't very practical."

I sank down onto the chaise beside him, and we were both silent for a while. I was angry, and I was trying to resist my urge to apologize to him. He tried to comfort me by patting my hand. "You couldn't wait to leave that house, Carmen. Don't you remember?"

I threw off his sympathetic hand and stood again. "I'm going swimming, and don't you dare come with me." My voice shook, and it was a little too loud. I felt like people all around me must be staring, as they should be. I had almost forgotten that I wasn't really speaking to another person. The noise of the beach may have prevented them from hearing my words, but they would have seen my gestures. Quickly, I thought of an excuse in case someone asked me what was going on. I would say that I was rehearsing for a play.

I hurried to the water, hoping again to find some measure of peace in its salty buoyancy. The waves were stronger than they had been earlier. I would have to pay more attention to them, which was good. The effort of concentration might distract me from my problems, but it didn't hold back my memories.

When I graduated from high school, I took on two new jobs, and left the one I'd had since I was sixteen. I didn't inform my parents in part to make it easier to hide my money from my father. If I was ever to get out of that house, he couldn't get a hold of any of my new higher income. He had already demanded that I pay more toward rent and expenses because I had turned eighteen, telling me, truthfully or not, that the government had decreased the amount of my mother's disability stipend when I became an adult.

Joella corroborated all of the lies I told my parents about spending time with friends who were getting ready to go away to their various colleges around the state. She even made up an excuse or two for me when I wasn't there to explain my own absences. I didn't tell her the truth either, but I know she guessed enough to understand that it was better that she didn't know too much.

I had to be out of the house before my friends disappeared, so I started looking for a suitable place to live right after graduation. There were potential roommates at both the housekeeping service and the restaurant. I took the first place that became available in a crowded apartment with three other cleaning women. The fourth was moving out at the beginning of August, and I began moving my belongings in before that. I carried one box at a time away from the house while Mom slept. Joella offered to help me carry more, but I couldn't risk trusting her with my destination. She was so upset by my leaving that she begged me to take her with me. I didn't listen to her desperate pleas. It was only in the last few years that I had given her more than the cell phone number that I gave to my folks, allowing her to reach out to as she had last Friday.

I felt it was necessary to get away from home and vital to keep my new life secret from them. I didn't care that it hurt my family. I spent as little time as I could with them, but I couldn't cut my ties completely, maybe, probably, because of my sister. I would not go to the house, but I met them for Mass and visited with them at church. At first they demanded my return and money, then they demanded to know where I lived and worked. Only after they stopped making demands would I agree to visit the house.

The first time I went back, it was a horrible mess. Joella had refused to do more than the most basic of household tasks. So every second or third Sunday, I cleaned for them and prepared meals that I froze for them to eat in between. Joella would help me do this, but she always protested. She swore that she could live in a sewer for the next seven years, but I couldn't let her do that.

The balance of our relationships changed. I gave them my telephone number after a few more months, but I usually called them every few days. Talking was easier when I set the time, usually just after dinner when they were sober. I didn't want to talk to them, not even to Joella, but by giving them a share of my time I avoided being subject to deeper inquiries. I said as little as possible, and listened, showing them honor and approval in every way I could. When they asked for money I didn't call again until we made it through a Sunday without another demand.

I closed Joella out too, because as she grew wilder and bolder she let some of my secrets slip, and though they may have been out of date, it still damaged the better relationship I was forging with our parents now that I was an adult. I didn't tell her where I worked at first, but she learned it from Arlene, one of my best friends from high school. I was not pleased the first time she showed up at the restaurant, and I threatened to hurt her if she let my secret out. Since then, though she had come to the salon to make sure she could really find me, no one else had come, and not even she had followed me home.

I was almost ready to leave the house when Joella spoiled my getaway. I had only been able to transfer about half of my belongings, but she panicked when she realized that I would be gone in a matter of days, and her moping turned to sobs. My mother heard her and stumbled to our room, where she saw me packing. Joella, full of guilt and misery, began to wail when she saw her. The noise reached my mother, even through her dulled senses, and she reacted by grabbing and tossing things from the box that stood closest to her. There was an odd, joyful look on her face. Jo and I picked up what we could and ran from the house, each with a heavy, open box.

"Don't follow me, Jo," I snapped at her. "You don't have to get in trouble too."

"I want to come with you."

"You can't! Go home!"

But she didn't. She stumbled behind me under the weight of the overflowing box. "I can't go back there. Not without you."

"I'll miss you too." I stopped and turned around so that we could speak normally. "But you're too young to leave home."

"Please, Carmen," she began.

I cut her off. "I can leave because I'm eighteen. An adult. I can sign a lease and vote and all that stuff." I was excited about my future, and I didn't want to think about what I was leaving, including her. I wouldn't let myself think about how her life would worsen after I left. I was the elder, and I'd taken the brunt of the punishments we had earned over the course of our lives. It seemed fair for me to blaze another trail for her to follow. Besides she was better at staying out of the way than I would ever be. I was ready to go out on my own. She wasn't. She was a small ten-year-old who hadn't even hit puberty yet. "You only have to wait 'til you're eighteen, Jo, and then it will be your turn."

She went with me all the way to the bus stop. When we got there we put down our boxes, and I began to arrange the contents. "Can I call you before I come back? I don't want that to happen next time."

"Of course," she muttered. Her face had dried, but she ran the palm of her hand over it to make sure. "I wish I was the big sister." She hugged me one last time. Then she bent to fold the box flaps under each other at each of the four corners. The bus arrived and she helped me hoist the heavy boxes up the steps.

I struggled with the two boxes all the way to my new home. They were too heavy to carry together, so when I transferred I had to make everyone wait while I fetched the second one, both getting on and off. My bed wasn't available yet in my new place, so I slept on the floor. I slept better than I ever had at home.

When my mother should have been asleep the next day I called home. "Is the coast clear?" I asked Joella.

"Don't bother, Carmen. Dad burned your stuff. He threw everything out the window last night, even some of my stuff. And then he built a big fire in the front yard where everyone could see. He even picked up some of the dead wood lying around in the yard to make sure it was hot enough to destroy everything."

CHAPTER SIX

The restaurant where I worked was called Dino's. It was a big family-friendly place owned by a big family. The second generation of Ghirellis ran it now, though the grandmother still came in to taste test the sauces. The third generation worked there too. Mario cooked with his mother in the back, and his cousin Connie managed the seating.

Connie had gotten pregnant when she was in high school, younger than Joella. Her son Brendan was six years old when I started working there. I hadn't wanted to have anything to do with him, but he was impossible to ignore. At first I thought there was something wrong with him. The way he wanted to talk to everyone who came in the restaurant seemed unnatural to me. While I had to be reminded every so often about smiling and showing interest in our patrons, he befriended them with ease. Watching him helped me to understand better how other people expected me to behave. The more I practiced friendliness, the more positive responses I received. People were nicer to me, and they left bigger tips. Though I still didn't like to share intimacies with other people, it wasn't as hard to share pleasantries. I could never have handled working at the salon without these skills.

Brendan's father was not involved in his life. I don't even know if he knew he had a son. I wondered how Connie's parents had reacted when they learned about her pregnancy. They could be brusque and high-tempered, the kind that screamed in angry moments, but they were also affectionate. I never heard anyone in the family complain despite all of the extra help the family gave Connie. And Brendan was treated the same way the other grandchildren were, except that his grandparents were just a little more interested in him because they knew him better.

I tried to picture my family six years in the future. It wasn't such a happy picture as the Ghirellis made. Joella's kid *could* win over my parents and settle into drinking and smoking with them. My folks might discover some scams that would allow them to collect charity money, since they were struggling to raise their bastard grandchild and support its deadbeat mother. Joella would work twenty hours a day to pay for everything, so my parents could keep all the charity money for themselves. They would need extra booze to sleep with a crying baby in the house.

There was no way that things would work out for Joella the way they had for Connie. Connie had a supportive family, and ours was worse than none.

For the millionth time today, I wished I could see into the future. How useful it would be to know what kind of person Justin was, that when he came home he would help Joella, that he would be willing and able to support her and their child. Not knowing him, I wasn't ready to consider him an ally, but even if he rejected Joella, I was certain somehow that he would not harm her.

I couldn't give my parents that kind of credit. They were spiteful, and whether they disowned Joella or not, they would try to tear her apart. They would remind her time and again of her debts to them. They would punish her. They might even punish me. Yet still, despite what other people might have considered insanity, I didn't think I could leave them to destroy themselves.

The strength of the current was only a part of why I found it difficult to relax. I bounced my pointed toes into the sand below, bobbing my shoulders in and out of the hills of water. I was out beyond the breakers, in my favorite spot, where I could swim but still touch. Farther from shore, a few surfers headed out to catch a long ride. Then a red and yellow canvas raft floated near me, unaffected by the side-to-side undercurrents.

"It worked for me because I was dedicated to Brendan," Connie explained from the top of the raft. She lay prone, dangling her legs off the back end and resting her cheek on her folded arms. Just as she had once before, she told me, "I had to work harder than I would have without him, and that meant I had to be away from him more than I wanted to be. I was torn in two so many times, doubting my choices and feeling selfish for going to school, being away from him, spending money I could have spent on him, not getting a better job because staying at the restaurant allowed my family to help me more than if I worked in an office somewhere. But I *knew* I had to do what I was doing. I needed to build a better future for both of us. I had to be away from him, but I refused to waste the time we had to be apart. Every moment away from him had to be well spent, because I could be missing an important event in his life. It wasn't good enough to tell him that I had to go; I had to be able to tell him that what I did was important."

My comment had been, "You're so lucky your family is ready to help," even six years ago thinking how that would never have happened in my own family.

"I thank God every day that I have such a wonderful family."

Now that my imagination had brought her to me, I asked her what seemed to be the most important question on my mind. "What would you do, Connie, if you had a family like mine?"

"Oh, God, I don't know..." she began. She raked her fingers through the water and gave a little kick to move her raft along with me in the current. "It's not easy, even with all the help we've had. I would have lost my mind with worry for Brendan, if I didn't have such confidence that he was being loved and reassured that his Mommy cared about him whenever I left him. No one can truly imagine having a child, Carmen. It's the ultimate, unending responsibility, and it's wonderful."

"How did your parents react when they learned you were expecting?"

"How do you think? Like everyone's parents," she answered offhandedly, as if it was a universal given.

"My folks would have beaten me 'til I miscarried," I growled back.

She stared at me for a minute. "Oh? So?" She knit her brows. "And you say your little sister's pregnant?"

"Right."

A wave rolled past us before she spoke again. I marveled at how her hair stayed dry.

"And you expect your parents are going to beat your sister until she loses the baby? So what the hell are you doing here? Shouldn't you go home and rescue her?"

Another wave came, and I didn't jump it, but stood dumbstruck, made less buoyant by my heavy heart. It seemed so simple when she said it, but I wasn't sure that I could save Joella. No, she had to be long gone from the house before she gave our parents the news, and if I was there, they would probably beat me too. It even occurred to me that she should tell them over the telephone or by letter instead of in person. Of course, none of that would help her if she ever wanted their forgiveness. They would hold our sneaking behind their backs against us right along with everything else.

"Carmen?"

"They don't know yet," I answered. "I have some time to decide what to do."

"Well, don't waste it, girl," she advised.

"That's why I came here, Connie. I needed to be away from everyone to open my mind up on this issue. As much as I want to help her, I'm not sure I can."

"Of course you can help her. It might be really hard, and you might have to make a lot of sacrifices, but it's not impossible. You might even like doing it." She kicked her raft around so that she could watch the waves coming at us, biding time, perceiving that I had nothing more to ask her now.

The waves were coming faster, stronger, and taller. I grew weary, from thinking rather than from swimming. I left Connie riding the waves and started toward the shore. When I looked back, I didn't see her. I shook my head, and dragged my legs through the thigh deep water. I wished I could imagine a raft for myself, so I could just ride into shore on the crest of one of those waves.

My knees were nearly buckled by a last, hard-hitting breaker. Then I was out, and, my head low, I glanced around at the ocean behind me. I heard the lifeguard's whistle and I scanned beyond the breakers to see some rowdy teenagers out in the rough water.

I felt a tap on my thigh, just above my knee, and I looked down to see a pair of big brown eyes under a floppy, blue, dinosaur printed hat. A smile appeared. I looked around. I looked down at him again. As I prepared to speak, I realized that I had returned his smile. "Where's your mom and daddy?"

He shrugged.

I made a slow visual search of the dry, bumpy sandscape. There were lots of families out on the shore today, but I couldn't tell which was his. "Let's move back from the water, Charlie. The waves are kind of rough."

He laughed at the name I gave him, but he agreed readily. He took my hand and pulled me out of the surf. Then he turned around again and pointed toward the water. He began to laugh again, an infectious giggle.

"What's so funny, Charlie?" I asked turning my gaze to follow the line from his finger. I saw Connie again, floating with the motion of the seas on her raft.

"Upside down lady!" Charlie's little voice squeaked with excitement.

As if at his command, Connie touched her hands to the canvas raft and threw her legs up into the air to do a handstand. "How the—" I began to question his knowledge of my singular vision.

He was still laughing and pointing, and when I looked beyond Connie I was relieved to see a woman doing stunts on her surfboard. Charlie clapped his hands together with delight. Staggered by that momentary detour from reality, I forgot to breathe until a lightheaded sensation reminded me. I regained control. Then I looked down at my new friend and asked, "Now, where's your family, Charlie?" It was easier to handle my concern for his welfare than for my sanity.

He pointed up onto the beach, and this time I noticed an older woman craning her neck to follow his movements. He pointed at her and said, "Gramma." I felt a surprising amount of relief that he had not been semi-abandoned. He turned to face the water again. "See surfing lady," he explained, fully confident that any adult would aid him in achieving his heart's desire.

"She's on her way out again. Let's watch her one more time before I take you back to your Grandma."

He turned and smiled and waved at his grandmother. She waved back. Her eye was on me too, and she was right to be cautious, especially if she had overheard any of my half of the conversation with Father Oleg. I scanned the area where I had been sitting, and not seeing Oleg, I turned my attention back to the ocean and the stunt surfer. Charlie put his warm, gritty hand in mine. His unquestioning affection was endearing. There were a few other people, some with cameras ready, standing with us waiting for the show.

My little friend pulled on my arm. I bent down, and before I had the chance to ask him what he wanted, he began to climb onto my back. I glanced at his grandmother for approval, and seeing her suppress a chuckle, I sensed her thoughts, "Better your back than mine," along with her acceptance. In turn, I helped him into position and stood again as quickly as I could without toppling. The surfer had caught the next wave, and it was a doozie, a tall green wall of water. Though I was beyond the water's edge, I still stepped backwards involuntarily as it came toward us. She inverted herself on the board, rode about thirty feet, and placed her feet back down again one at a time to ride in the usual manner.

As I turned to take my little friend back to his grandmother, his grandfather, who was building a sandcastle with two older children, got up and came to take him from me. "Looks like you made a new friend, Billy."

"Charlie," Billy answered, assertively pointing at his own chest.

"Ho ho, you are?" the grandfather laughed, seeming to understand exactly how Billy had gotten a new name. "If you would tell people your name, then you wouldn't have to change it all the time," he advised. He held out his hand to me, "I'm Jim, and Charlie here is my grandson Billy."

"Nice to meet you," I said, politely shaking sandy hands. No harm, because neither of us made the other any messier. "I'm Carmen."

"You're welcome to join our project team, señorita. We're constructing a fine castle today."

And so I spent the next forty-five or so minutes on my knees in the border sand having a blast and could have forgotten my problems if they had regarded something other than families and children. Jim's wife came down to suggest it was time for everyone to come into the shade, and after that they started to get ready to go home. From under their umbrella, where they brushed off sand and packed to go, they waved good-bye to me. I waved back. Then I took a long drink and sat in my own shady spot. It would have done little good to ask the advice of such people, for they would never quite have been able to believe that families like mine really existed, and their reassurances would have left me feeling more isolated than ever.

In the first moments of my encounter with Billy, I had had to work to calm the terror released by thinking that he had been able to see Connie. He could only have seen her if he had also been a denizen of my mind, and I was sure I would have failed every known test of sanity if I began to converse with imaginary strangers.

His being real was far more persuasive than any fictional representation of the child in my sister's womb I could have created. His charm and that of the older children, which I could never have imagined, had eased my concerns. The grandparents were interested and engaged; I'd had the opportunity to observe a family as it should function. They made it look like it was a simple thing to care about each other. Maybe I too could learn to be kind to my sister and her child, even if I failed as a daughter.

Who knew? Perhaps Justin's family was like the one on the beach. It was possible. I had heard that most families work very hard to protect their children from the impact of the parents' mistakes. Maybe this was the kind of family I should model.

I didn't have the energy to talk to anyone. After such a pleasant hour, I thought I should have felt better about things, but I couldn't stop the sad feelings, tenseness, and even anger from building up in me again.

In my weakness, I must have invited Father Oleg to return, though I had wished he would stay away wherever it is such people go when they slip one's mind. His arm went around my shoulders. "Go out and have fun tonight, Carmen. You deserve it. And the boy will understand if you tell him what's going on," Father Oleg said, trying to encourage me.

"I can't tell him what's going on!" I snapped back.

"You don't have to tell him all the details. Just tell him you've been trying to make a tough decision. He'll honor your privacy."

"He'll ask questions that I shouldn't answer."

"You eased up at lunch, didn't you?"

I nodded. I wanted to cry. Then suddenly, without thinking about it, I threw off his comforting arm and scooted away from him. "And where do you get off touching me like that?"

He moved quickly to the chair opposite from me, not apologizing, but studying me closely. "I'm sorry," he said at last. "I thought it would make you feel better."

I aimed a low growl at him.

"You touch people all the time," he began. I was sure he was going to turn his degree in psychology to use, and I wanted no part of it.

"I touch. You don't," I said firmly. "You are the customer, get it? You don't touch the stylist. You wouldn't touch your doctor, would you? Or your priest?"

He shook his head slowly indicating that he understood, but he was still thinking about it. "No," he said, "I suppose I wouldn't. But I do touch my friends. And I thought we were friends, and you aren't cutting my hair. And I guess that's a good thing," he added, smiling to show me that he intended to use humor against my anger, "because if you were you'd have scissors and razors in your hands."

"Keep that in mind next time you're in my chair," I said, lightening only a few degrees.

"I might not sit in your chair again."

"That might be wise."

"What's gotten into you, Carmen?" he asked in sweeter tone.

I didn't feel like being cajoled. I crossed my arms and pouted.

"Come on," he urged. "Tell me what's going on. Are you just nervous about your date?" He looked at me; I turned my head trying to ignore him. It was impossible. "So, what's new in that brain of yours?"

"Nothing," I huffed.

"You were having fun with that family, weren't you? Are you jealous?"

"Of course I am," I said, smiling thinly. Maybe he'd stop badgering me if I gave him an answer.

"They seemed nice, but…"

"Oh, pray tell me, what could possibly be the problem with them?"

"They are Satan worshippers."

"Right! And how do you figure that?" I urged him to continue.

"Did you see what the grandmother was reading?"

Perplexed, I answered, "She was reading *The DaVinci Code*."

"See, evil, heretical, sinful, anti-Church, and conniving. Devious too. And that sandcastle was shaped like a pentagram."

"It was not!" My mood was shifting.

"It was."

"It was not." Still, I weakened. "I thought it was round. But even if it was? So what? That old fort in Eastmont is star shaped. Were our ancestors Satan worshippers?"

"As a matter of fact, some of them were, but that's another issue."

"Where do you come up with this stuff?"

"Everything I say comes from you."

"Then why does it keep surprising me?"

"I guess you have a highly compartmentalized mind."

"Great. I guess I'll never walk alone."

He looked pleased, which amazingly didn't further my irritation. "You never do, my daughter. You never do."

CHAPTER SEVEN

"Didn't even look at it," I griped to Father Oleg as I picked my magazine up out of my bag and dropped it in again without even glancing at the gorgeous, famous actress on the cover.

"I flipped pages while you were practicing your aunting skills. Can't say as it excited me much either," he replied, ignoring the fact that I was trying to lay the blame for everything that was going on in my head on him. He was back on his own lounge chair holding a cold drink.

"I wanted to read it," I said with an impatient sigh. "But I need to go inside now."

"So go." He made no movement.

I felt abandoned. Impatiently I snapped, "Are you planning to get sun stroke?"

"Ha!" he grunted back. With a superior expression, Oleg took a long drink, watching me as I collected my belongings.

I was done before he lowered his cup again. Then I realized that I was thirsty too, so I pulled my water bottle out and drank for nearly as long as he had. I capped the bottle and dropped it into my bag.

"I'm trusting you to keep me out of danger." He watched me with intense interest. "As a matter of fact, I think it would be nice if you'd imagine my legs being the way God made them. I'd love to dump this old cane in the trash," he

85

added, pointing at one of the steel refuse barrels. He didn't appear to be thinking about what he said; all of his attention was on me. I found it curious that my own mental image paid so much attention to its source. I guess I was more self-centered than I had previously believed.

Then he changed the subject. "What will you do if Dennis touches you?"

"Huh?"

"Come on. After that display earlier, I can't help but wonder. What if he touches you?"

"That's none of your business," I snapped, frowning. I wadded the towels and chucked them toward the foot of the chair for the staff to clear away; I'd watched Billy's grandparents do this, so I was sure it was the proper procedure.

"Granted, but let's say he takes your hand to help you with a step or he pushes your chair in at supper? Worst of all, what if he asks you to dance with him?"

"Oh, get real!"

"Me?"

"Men never do that. I mean, not regular guys. I'll be alright."

"And this Dennis fellow isn't a gentleman?" Oleg pushed himself up to standing. "Dear me, Carmen," he clucked. "Why are you going to go out with him if you think he's got no class?"

"I didn't say that," I replied, defending my choice. I rolled my eyes. "I just don't think he'll do that chair pushing business."

"Maybe not, but you should be ready in case he does. Or if you go to a place where the waiters wait on you hand and foot. You'll have a hard time explaining it if you freak out the way you did earlier."

"I'll insist on fast food. Does that satisfy you?" I snapped back, sensitive at the mention of my foibles.

"Not in the least. Not for a first date dinner. He has to take you to a restaurant with menus and servers. If he doesn't, he's a total loser." He sounded completely certain. "I should know. I never had much success with women. I mean, I'm hotter now than when I was in the game."

"Hotter?"

"It's the unapproachable thing," he shrugged pseudo-modestly.

"Yeah." I tried to keep a straight face. "That must be it." Then I added, "I'm going." I turned and walked away from our little island of shade without looking back to see him hurriedly hobbling after me.

It didn't take him long to catch up with me. "Where do you think he's going to take you tonight? Did he drop any hints?"

"No."

"Do you know what you're going to wear?"

"Well, it's this dress or my shorts. I didn't pack anything else."

"Oh, yeah, right. And don't worry about me. I'll keep myself occupied while you're off with the man. The hotel has plenty of nooks to explore."

"As long as you don't do your exploring where I am."

"I will turn around and go the other way if I see you."

"Good. Thanks."

"I guess I should be grateful that you've let me come along as much as you have."

I smirked and almost said, "My pleasure," but I knew the attitude behind my expression would hurt his feelings. Oleg couldn't help being the way he was. The real Father Oleg was much like this imagined one, but he wasn't so intrusive.

I had built into him the very most irreverent and annoying aspects of his personality.

We walked quietly most of the way. When we were close to the pool yard, he told me that he was going to take a look to see if Dennis was still there. "I want to check him out." I shrugged to him in parting, and continued on my way. "I'll suggest he wear a necktie on your date," he called to me.

Leaving him behind, I pictured turning and shouting back, "If he could hear you, and if he brought one."

I was relieved that even my imagination was going to let me walk through the hotel lobby alone. I dallied in front of the shop windows, thinking, almost wishing that I felt free to drop fifty dollars or probably more on something new and cute to wear tonight. It wasn't really much of a temptation, because all of expensive items I saw looked like they were made for old people, as was so often the case. Not many people under forty could afford them, but then we younger people didn't need to be as particular about what we wore either.

I was fascinated by the elegant public spaces. Never having stayed in a hotel before, I had been completely unprepared for the range of amenities under the roof of The Neptune. I knew that I had yet to discover all kinds of facilities contained in this glamorous tower of hospitality. My room was an attractive and comfortable haven, but I found the balconies and terraces, the shops, restaurants, and other guest facilities far more interesting. The people too, so varied and active, were intriguing. I wanted to learn what they were doing and understand why they enjoyed it. They seemed so free, and I was puzzled because I felt freer when I was with them.

It was nearly five o'clock when I returned to my room. Though I knew it had been time to get out of the sun, I wasn't thrilled about having two hours to kill before going out again. Showering and dressing wouldn't take much time. Flipping through the pages of my magazine no longer appealed to me the way it had when Oleg was bugging me. I'd begun to put some pressure on myself to make a success out of my evening with Dennis. I felt an odd eagerness to see him again.

I caught a glimpse of my reflection on the base of one of the brass lamps. I looked hot, flustered, and worried until I smiled. I looked pretty despite the extra roundness provided by the curving metal. I played with my messy hair and practiced smiling.

"I guess I can watch TV if I'm ready early," I said aloud. With only a twitch of guilt I thought that killing time by watching television would be a better way to prepare for a date than thinking about my sister's problems. Better yet, I could explore more of the hotel and burn off energy.

My skin was sticky and gritty, and it felt raw from exposure to the beach elements, especially because I'd gotten sunburned. I hung my clothes on the back of a chair to air and took fresh undergarments with me into the bathroom. I left the door open, dropped my swimsuit into the sink to rinse, and started the shower. I stood under the nozzle allowing the sand to slide down from my head to my heels and on to muck up the floor of the bathtub. It felt nearly as wonderful to wash the sand and salt away as it had to accumulate them during my time on the beach.

My bliss was swept away in an instant as my mother, already ranting and red-faced, tore open the curtain. "Damn you, Carmen! You know better than to come inside without rinsing at the tap outside. You've left a trail through the house, from the door to the tub. You'll plug up the pipes!"

"It's a hotel, Mom," I said replied, my control vanishing in the very instant she appeared. I tried to steady myself and will her away. I couldn't do it. Curiosity as much as anything drew me into the memory.

If my mother had ever needed to stop ranting to draw breath, I might have been able to suggest that she pause to take a deep one. They say it helps a person relax and keep things in perspective. My mother, however, never seemed to need to gather her breath, and this version of her exaggerated this ability to the point that it seemed one phrase overlapped another as they poured from her mouth. "This isn't some fucking hotel, young lady, where someone's going to clean up after you. This is your own stinking house, and you are going to clean every grain of sand out of here before you clean off your own flabby ass." She grabbed me roughly by the arm and pulled me over the side of the tub, bruising my shins and spilling wet sand onto the floor. She turned the water off impatiently, and then she yanked my arm again, pulling me, still naked and dripping wet, behind her all the way to the front door.

I hugged myself, shivering, until she shoved the broom and pan into my hands. "I'll warm you if you don't start cleaning up this mess!" I understood her threat. Mom would take the broom to my bare bottom if I didn't put it to use quickly enough. She was a big woman, and I was a short, round eight-year-old. I did my best to keep her from touching me again, knowing her next effort would be much more painful than the first. I swept the hall, and then I mopped it. While it dried, I began to push the heavy vacuum cleaner over the parts of the carpet I had passed over on my way to the bath. I was still naked, but I was warm now from the work, the anger, and the embarrassment.

My mother, a gloating mountain, watched me, arms crossed over her bosom and a sneer of victory on her face. She did nothing to prevent Joella from crawling through the places I had already cleaned. Jo cried for me to stop and play with her, frightened by the sternness of Mom's voice and the wheeze of the vacuum cleaner (I couldn't push it unless I set the height adjustment to its highest level, which did a very poor job of sucking up the damp sand.). To make things worse, clumps of sand dropped from the wrinkles of Jo's diaper and between her tiny toes. The cleanup seemed to go on forever, but all the time that I worked at it, I promised myself that the next time we played in our neighbors' sandbox, I would make sure both of us were well rinsed and dried before we came inside the house.

My mother was pleased with herself. She had been able to punish me and delegate a good amount of housework in one easy step. It was a win-win situation for her. It wasn't always as easy to shift the work to me, though as I grew older, and wanted to avoid punishment, I voluntarily took on more of it. I taught Joella too, and as Mom's abilities declined we kept the peace at home by anticipating her wishes and those of our father. Mom never showed that she noticed, and we never altogether avoided her fits and fists, but the effort was worth it.

The saddest truth of our early life was that Joella and I were never able to form a strong enough bond to protect each other. We fought our battles individually. Though I never thought she was old enough or strong enough to look after herself, I didn't make much of an effort to stand up for her. When I did try, she resented it and defended herself, even when I told her it was time to be quiet or hide. She took more than she should have from my mother. So did I, but I was quicker to scurry into retreat and try to figure ways to work around her. Jo would take whatever it was my mother threw at her. I wondered if she had gotten smarter after I moved out, and could only conclude that she must have. No one could keep taking that kind of treatment and keep her health and her sanity as Joella seemed to have done.

We might have been able to protect each other. We might have been able to distance ourselves from our parents. By the time I thought that Jo understood this, however, I was ready to leave and to be gone and to forget. I had put the anger behind me, I had put the pain behind me, I had put my responsibility to Joella behind me, and I had convinced myself that I owed my parents the kind of respect that most parents have earned.

Yet here I was, thinking about what I should do for Joella for less than a day, and already memories were resurfacing. As far back as I had pushed them, now that I had opened one room the other doors were opening too. Reality may bend, but it doesn't go away.

The showerhead must have been faulty. While I stood with my hands on the tiles, the water running over me and into every bend and pore of my body, the stream turned to a trickle. And the cold I felt in the absence of the warm water roused me from my stupor. I felt like I had been gone from my body for hours. The washcloth and the soap were still dry. Hurriedly, I turned on the flow again and scrubbed my shivering nakedness of the sweat and filth from that spring day all those years ago. I shook from more than the cold until after I was dry. I put on my underwear. Then I went into the room to check the time. It was after six o'clock already. I dropped onto the bed, fatigued, and looked at my shriveled fingers and toes.

"Too bad I can't paint my nails after all," I said to myself, reminded by my bleached nails of Father Oleg's earlier comment. I thought of his pushy behavior with a pleasant sentimentality now after my most recent mental ambush. I forced a smile and stretched, trying to improve my spirits. I may not have brought any nail polish with me, but I had met an attractive young man, who I had the feeling would be incredibly shocked if he understood me. Although I didn't think I would be ready to share what was going on with even a long time best friend, I did deserve to have fun and friends. For now Father Oleg was probably the best I should hope for. Maybe the real priest would know how to handle a misfit like me.

I got up and paced around the room, wanting a complete return to the physical moment. The movement had a calming effect. I began to warm where I had been cold and cool where I had been hot. I got out my aloe to spread on my sunburn, and then I went into the bathroom to put on my clothes.

My skin was a warm pink, and a new batch of freckles erupted over most of me even as I watched. I combed my wet hair. There wasn't much else to do. My shoulder length auburn hair would be my main asset, as usual, but I was more gifted with a hairdryer than the average girl, and I could create a different look with the very same hair Dennis had seen at midday.

CHAPTER EIGHT

I finished getting ready and left my room with time to spare before I expected Dennis. It felt too confining inside, so I went outside onto one of the terraces that girded the lower floors of the hotel. The whole area was in deep shade, though the sky was still bright. Like the first star of the evening, pale lights began weakly to twinkle in the trees. This day was drawing to its end.

I went to the wall and looked out over the ocean. The wind caressed my face. It was invigorating, even soothing. I pressed my hands against the cooling stone, arching my back and breathing cool, salty air deep into my lungs. Still processing my memories, I altered their form so that I could be aware of them without having to live through them again.

When I turned my head, I found Oleg at my side. He leaned against the wall beside me, dressed for the evening in his everyday black trousers and tunic. "You're doing better, Carmen." He was referring to the way I had jumped away from him earlier. In a gentle tone, he added, "Thank you for confiding in me."

My reaction was almost detached, just a nod. Remaining calm, I produced a mere hint of a smile to indicate my own gratitude. He disappeared. I lingered until I decided it was time to go back to my room to meet Dennis.

I was at my door when Dennis approached. He called a greeting before I saw him, his voice choppy with laughter, his eyes scanning me approvingly. "Are you ready, Carmen? Or do you plan on further outdoing yourself?"

With a blush I responded. "No, I'm ready. Just need to get my purse."

He waited, leaning against the doorframe. When I came out, he asked about my afternoon, and I told him, "I helped build a sandcastle with some children, and I got a sunburn."

"Ew. Hope it's not bad. With that fair skin, Carmen, you need be extra careful."

"I should be," I admitted. "You're lucky to have a darker complexion. That must protect you a little."

He shrugged. "A bit, I guess. One of my grandmothers is Venezuelan."

"That's interesting."

"Maybe that's why I like Spanish girls." The elevator opened at the lobby. "I like building sandcastles too. How did yours turn out?"

"Well, um, it *was* fun to build. This adorable little boy latched onto me 'cause he wanted to see this lady that was doing handstands on her surfboard, and then his grandfather invited me to join the fun. There were three little kids. I've never done anything like that before."

"Wow! Sounds like you had a great afternoon."

"It was pretty good," I agreed, pushing back memories of my memories. "So, how was the pool?"

"Nice. You should use it before you go home. It's big, and I had a great swim." He gestured for me to go through the revolving door first, and he followed me outside. A long awning came out from the hotel entrance to the car lane and extended in a semi-circle over the sidewalk both ways to the street. There was carpeting on the walk near the door, presumably to keep the sand outside. Hotelmen in uniforms nodded to us as we turned off the brick pavement to stepping stones through a miniature, manicured jungle, taking a short cut to the street.

"I hope you're hungry. I was down to see the concierge about places to eat, and the one I selected sounds like it has generous portions."

"Where are we going?" I asked.

"A Brazilian place. I hope it's good." He gritted his teeth a little, showing his insecurity.

We turned right at the end of the garden path, and continued on to the next corner where we crossed the street. It was a short two blocks further inland before we turned left on the near side of the street. A few doors down, Dennis slowed his steps, and I followed suit. "This is the place: Brasilia's."

I looked quickly at the sign and nervously at Dennis.

"You aren't a vegetarian, are you?" he asked, the strength in his voice trickling away.

"No. I like meat. It's just, it looks expensive. Are you sure?"

He broke into a wide grin. "Oh, that's it! You're a gem, Carmen! Don't worry about that. I saw the menu." He offered me his arm, and I touched his sleeve with my fingertips in an effort to be polite. He accepted the gesture, so it must have been close to correct. We went up the stairs, and he withdrew his arm to open the door for me. He moved us through these polite exchanges without any drama. It wasn't as strange as I expected. Maybe it was easier because he offered courtesy rather than forcing it on me. There's a difference. "I mean, I don't eat like this every day," he continued. His tone was light and chatty. "But why not—for a special occasion? Of course, I may not be able to eat anything other than my ice cream tomorrow."

Remembering some of the things that Father Oleg had said this afternoon, I stopped myself from making any further arguments. I could almost picture the look on my priest's face when he learned where we had gone. "The boy almost got it right. It's not quite romantic enough for a girl, now is it? But then it could be you don't want a romantic setting."

The interior was dim, and the air was rich with spices and grilled meat. The setting was definitely masculine: beamed ceiling, stone floor, raised booths with steps up to the seats, and air, smoky from the cooking. To one side of the entry hall there was a bar where men drank, burned tobacco, and watched sports on a choice of televisions. I did no more than glance to see that it was there. The whole place was foreign to me.

I looked around, feeling transported, as the host led us to our table. It almost seemed like we had gone outdoors to a barbecue on the terrace of a ranch on the fringes of the Amazon rain forest, except that I'm sure we were more comfortable inside the air conditioned dining room.

"I think I could be happy just to chew on the air in this place." His voice came out no louder than his deep, inhaling breath. He seemed ill at ease, and I guessed it was because he wasn't sure that this had been a good choice for a first date with a feminine girl.

I didn't mind. We were in a strange town, so every place would have been something of a gamble. "I know what you mean," I said, but I found the aromas were stimulating rather than slaking my hunger. "Do you suppose they charge by the breath?"

My joke seemed to lift his tension. "Remember I saw the menu. You can breathe in as much as you like. It's not too smoky for you?"

"No, I'm fine," I replied.

We were shown to a booth. I was relieved after Father Oleg's sermon earlier that there were no chairs to be moved. After the host left us, I whispered to Dennis that I had half-expected him to speak to us in Spanish.

"Portuguese," Dennis said automatically, and then he looked like he wanted to take the word back.

"Huh?"

"Sorry," he blushed. "The Brazilians speak Portuguese, not Spanish." He looked more bothered about having made the correction than I felt for having erred.

"Oops." I tried to laugh at my mistake. "I'm learning a lot today."

"I hope I'm not being pedantic."

"I don't think so," I replied, not wanting to admit that I didn't really know what that meant either. I was sure that he was being nice to me. I opened my menu, but I looked around the room to find something else to talk about so that he would relax. There was plenty of activity, with diners carrying plates from a buffet line and men carrying spitted meat from table to table. As I turned my attention back to the table, Dennis caught my eye. I smiled. "I think this is going to be fun."

"Shall we get a bottle of red wine? Do you have a favorite?"

"Actually, I'd just like water, please."

"Okay," he responded slowly. "That's it? Coffee after?"

"Maybe." I turned my attention back to the menu, but Dennis put his hand out to stop me.

"It's a buffet, Carmen. I'll take care of the ordering."

"Okay. Sure." I closed the menu and put it down again.

"You don't mind if I have a glass, do you?"

"Oh, no, why would I?"

"Well, you know, sometimes." He stopped at a loss to explain. "Sometimes it's awkward. I don't have to have wine. I'm not a big drinker, really." He looked apologetic. "Oh, never mind."

His discomfort made me feel guilty. "I don't mind at all. Go ahead." This didn't seem to reassure him enough, so I added, "I've never developed a taste for it."

He looked like he couldn't figure out what to say next. If he offered to let me try some of his, he'd feel like he was pushing it on me. If he didn't offer, he'd feel like a bad host. I understood as well as if Father Oleg were sitting beside me explaining it. It seemed better to offer a little more of the truth. "My parents are both heavy drinkers," I said quickly. "I'm afraid that if I try it I might like it too well."

"Oh!" he cried apologetically. "I'm sorry. I didn't mean to make you feel like I was pressuring you."

"You didn't," I said in as reasonable and calm a tone as I could manage. "I just thought it was better to explain. I thought I might be causing a manners dilemma. I honestly don't care what you drink. You aren't driving or going to work tomorrow. If you turn ugly-drunk, I can find my way back to the hotel alone." I was serious, and meant just to clear the air, but he started to laugh. At first I found it irritating, but as I realized he meant no insult I relaxed and waited for his amusement to abate, even coming to smile with him.

"I like you!" he announced with enthusiasm. He sat back farther into his seat. How was this conversation going to move forward? He nodded. "You've got a very no-nonsense way of looking at things. It's refreshing."

"You just caught me on an off day," I said, playing along.

"Oh, so you're usually more convoluted than today? Tell me, are you often held captive by your imagination?"

I shrugged. "*It* has been a little more direct today than most."

He smiled again, restraining another laugh. "What's so special about today?"

"I met you."

"No fair! You were off and running long before I interrupted your list making. Besides, that was my line."

"Not anymore." I sat up straighter. "Today has just been really strange. Up and down."

"I'm glad you didn't have to wait for the demons to clear out of the restaurant before we could eat."

"We haven't eaten yet," I reminded him.

"But," he tipped his head toward the approaching waiter, "we soon will."

Our table was set with large plates and tall glasses of ice water when we returned from the buffet with small dishes of bread and vegetables. A carver approached us and offered to slice roasted beef for us, followed soon after by another with lamb. After they moved on, Dennis returned us to our previous conversation. "I'd be nervous about drinking if either of my parents drank too much. You know how they say, 'like father, like son'."

"I think it works that way for mothers and daughters too."

"Do you live with your folks?"

"No."

"I detect a note of finality. They must charge rent."

"Way more than I can afford."

"I lived with mine even after I finished school for a while. They never charged me, you know. They just asked me to keep up certain things around the house and not to stay out too late. It was all about being considerate. They understood that I was an adult, and they weren't about trying to cramp my style."

"That sounds reasonable. Maybe they could adopt me."

As usual, he laughed a little too quickly. I chalked it up to nerves. Dennis wanted very badly for me to have a good time. He tried too hard to please me, but for the most part I found the attention more enjoyable than I ever would have expected, though I wouldn't want to be treated that way all of the time. This was the kind of thing that would probably smooth out on its own as we got to know each other better, if we got to know each other better, and I was thinking that I would like to. He was nice, and it took little effort for us to get along. It was only when I knocked over my water glass that I found myself in difficulty.

With a bursting, "Ho there!" Dennis jumped aside to avoid receiving a lap full of ice water. He chuckled as he caught my glass and righted it before it rolled off the table. "You've had too much to drink, Carmen. No more water for you."

I paled, failing to see the humor in the situation. In fact, his face seemed to fade away from me as I was carried back into the past again.

I was ten years old, and Joella three. I was carrying a glass in each hand from the kitchen to the dinner table when I tripped. The glasses hit the floor just before my bottom landed in the middle of broken glass and curdling milk. I struggled to get up without further injury. My hands bled, and my bottom, still impaled, was in agony.

"Look at the mess you made, you idiot klutz." My father's voice was mocking. His calm tone gave away his lack of surprise.

Joella began to cry. My mother rushed away from the stove to look. With her sharp hearing she would have heard everything: the jump rope Joella was dragging across the floor, my gasp as I lost my balance, the handle of the jump rope hitting the floor after my father dropped it, the glass shattering, and me landing with a hard thud. She stopped at the door between the kitchen and the living room, grease dripping from the spoon in her hand. "Why are you bawling?" she snapped at Jo. "It's Carmen's fault this time. Shut up."

Joella tried hard to obey and ended up hiccoughing from the stress.

Then Mom turned to me. "How the hell did you manage this?"

"I tripped," was the only answer I could manage. I looked around at the floor for evidence, but I didn't want to incriminate Joella so I said no more. I was only just figuring out what had happened. I displayed my bleeding hands. "My bottom hurts," I gulped, hoping to banish my tears.

She made a low noise, like a growl. "Don't just stand there waiting for me to straighten this out. You made this mess, you clean it up. If you leave this on the floor, there'll be a stain. If we lose our deposit back on this measly house, Christ, I'll have your hide."

For years I thought that we would be kicked out of our home if I didn't do a good enough job cleaning up each mess for which I was held responsible. Of course, my folks still lived in that same rental house, and now I understood that if the owners cared about the condition of their property, they would have long since evicted my family. At that time, however, those words frightened and motivated me, and my mother knew it.

"Go on, Stupid. I'll punish you after we eat. The faster you're done the less time I'll spend tanning your blubber butt." She didn't stop ranting until I'd returned with the mop and broom, dallying just long enough to remove the blade from my backside. That made the bleeding worse, but I couldn't do anything about that. I set to work picking up the broken glass, warning Jo to keep her bare feet away, and Mom returned to the stove, her spoon still dripping grey grease. "Damn you, Carmen, you made our dinner burn."

She continued her tirade from the kitchen. The first thing she did was pour another glass of whiskey for Dad, which she sent to him in Joella's shaking, little hands. He was content to watch me work without comment or sympathy. He had raised his feet when the spill hit the floor, and he kept them up, not to make my job easier but for his own safety.

I barely even dared to think about how he had caused this mess. No matter how cautious I was, he still managed tricks like this with regularity, and as angry as she got over the messes that were made, Mom never hinted that she was aware of his involvement. That omission spoke volumes to me even at the age of ten. If she hadn't gotten so upset, I might have believed they planned these things together, but she was too stressed to have known it was coming. He enjoyed aggravating her. There was a fine difference between the proactive nature of my father and the reactive workings of my mother. She knew that he was devious, that he liked to see her yell and bluster at us, to keep us timid and separate, but she never complained to him for his part in it. Not once did she lay the blame where it belonged. He watched the three of us like a psychologist studies the behavior of frantic rats trying to repair his destruction.

Mom's reactions were probably the most interesting. Excited and red with the exertion of yelling, hating the chaos that children bring to a home, she redirected the hatred she must feel for him at her daughters.

I couldn't help but wonder if I should feel sorry for her, stuck in her manipulative eddy. But how could I feel sorry for her? How could I feel sympathy for anyone? Even for Joella?

"Carmen?"

There was a gentle tap on the hand I was using to wipe the spill from the table, and I quickly retracted my hand, sopped napkin and all.

"Are you okay, Carmen?" It was Dennis.

I was suddenly, safely back in the present. No one would punish me for spilling my water glass here in this restaurant. The waiter would take care of the mess, just as I had done when I served meals at Dino's. Looking into my lap bashfully, I placed the dripping napkin on the table, near the edge where the waiter would be sure to see it and bring me a fresh one.

Dennis sounded concerned. "What's wrong?"

I blinked, and looked up at him. "Nothing," I lied.

"You sure? Your imagination isn't ganging up on you again, now, is it?"

Tense and wondering how he could see through me so easily, I forced a laugh. "It's just an old habit. My mother was always worried about watermarks on the table." Close enough to the truth. My stomach twisted. I looked at my plate, which still held most of the food I had selected. I swallowed down the bile. I wanted to run to the restroom, but I knew that Dennis would be more worried about me if I had such a strong reaction. He would know if I vomited. No matter how much better it might make me feel, it wouldn't be worth upsetting him the way I was sure it would. I took a deep breath and picked up a chunk of ice from the table, hoping it looked like an absent-minded gesture. In my lap I rubbed the ice between my shaking palms. It helped.

"I think I'll submit an article to one of those tabloid rags: 'Hydrophobic Girl Visits Beach'," he said.

Still caught in my quicksand memory, I was slow to respond. "So that's why you're buying me ice cream and supper? You're a journalist in disguise."

"Definitely not. But, really, Carmen, are you okay?"

"Yes." I smiled a moment too late. "Of course I'm okay."

He put his hand across the table, inviting me to put mine into it for comfort. I pretended not to see it, and he slowly turned it palm down and bent his elbow, removing his sympathy to a distance I could tolerate. I began to relax, despite the fact that it was becoming increasingly difficult not to admit what was going on to Dennis. He seemed so kind and concerned that it bothered me to lie to him—and not just because I could see that he could tell when I lied. I so badly needed to talk to someone, and some instinct *almost* made me want to open up to him.

When the waiter came, he took away the wet napkin and soon returned with a clean one and another glass of water. The dark blotches on the tablecloth were already lightening. I looked at Dennis, who seemed only to care how I felt. The ice had long since melted, so I put one hand up on the table again, and gradually he worked his over near it again, leaving it a couple of inches away, not touching, but close enough to show solidarity. I didn't have room in my brain to wonder why he bothered to make such an effort over me.

"I've been preoccupied," I confessed. I managed to keep my voice calm, though I was closer to breaking my silence than I had ever been. I was sure that Dennis wouldn't ask too many questions; he'd know not to cross into matters which were too personal. Even Joella and I had never discussed my mother's tirades or excessive punishment between us. We didn't want to admit that we'd accepted these things. We only ever referred to our parents in a distant kind of way. We didn't look into each other's eyes. We never voiced our envy for the families of our friends. We each handled our parental relationships alone. Speaking to her would have meant admitting that I understood what was happening to me and that I was allowing it to happen to her as well.

I barely allowed myself to think about this or to remember these things. I wanted it all well behind me. Only for today, I vowed, would I be this open. This was the act of daring I had promised of myself this morning. I had let go of my discipline, and I'd lost control, but I would rein it all in tomorrow.

Worse than admitting this to each other was admitting it to other people. Neither Joella nor I wanted to be seen as children of hatred with no chance of redemption. My best chance was to aim for a neutral life, never growing close enough to other people for them to know my secrets and the darkness in my soul. And suddenly I thought about Joella, now carrying a baby inside of her. She must not be permitted to procreate, for she could only bring another person like us into the world. Surely it would be safer for this babe to skip life on earth and go straight to God's loving arms; wouldn't an abortion be the kindest act that his mother could perform for him?

"I've been trying to work out a problem, Dennis," I explained. "It's not something I can discuss, really. But when I space out, it's like some new aspect of the situation is presenting itself. I'm sorry. I guess it wasn't fair of me to come out with you tonight. I don't suppose I'm the best companion."

"Well, I wish there was a way I could help you, but I'll try not to put any more pressure on you." He ran his hands over the smooth tablecloth. "And as for the quality of your companionship, I've no right to complain. I knew you were distracted when I asked you to join me, and I'm still enjoying being with you. Let's at least finish our dinner, and then if you want to call it a night, I'll understand."

"Sure," I said slowly. I couldn't help but wonder if he'd found a polite way to dump me off early, as genuine as he seemed about enjoying our time together. I wished I could just live in this moment, as he was, and enjoy hanging out with him, because as far as I could tell, he was one of the nicest people I'd ever met.

"Only one hitch," he added.

"What's that?"

"May I ask for your phone number? Your home number, I mean, not your room here." He smiled. He must have been reading my mind, and I almost wished he could read my mind when I lost control of it. "Please." His forehead wrinkled and his voice pitched high, he made an expectant, begging face. It was irresistible.

"Sure," I answered, relieved and trying not to reply too speedily. "I'd be glad to."

CHAPTER NINE

I thought our evening would draw to a close quickly after that. Instead, it took on a new life. I hadn't expected Dennis to be nervous asking me about future contact—after all, I was the one with issues—yet he relaxed noticeably too. I think that he picked up on my lack of dating experience early on, and that may have explained some of his generosity. We ate slowly and talked a lot. When we were through with our food, Dennis ordered coffee to cap off our out-sized meal. Conversation grew easier, as it often does over a warm beverage.

"You really have to leave tomorrow?" he asked as we waited for the waiter to return with the bill and his credit card.

"Y'I do. I didn't arrange for any time away from work. In fact, this trip was a whim."

"So you just needed to break away from it all to work something out?"

"Yeah." I ducked my head hoping to avoid discussing this.

Apparently that was invitation for another question. "Carmen? I mean, I know I shouldn't pry, but you aren't mixed up in something bad are you?"

"What?" My head jerked up.

"I mean," he started, worried enough about me to risk pushing the limits of politeness. "I mean, you are obviously really bothered by this, whatever it is. Has someone tried to hurt you?"

I didn't respond quickly enough, and the look of concern on his face intensified. I was actually somewhat relieved that his concerns were of such a simple nature. It meant I could give him a direct, truthful answer, without elaborating. Knowing that his credulity was being severely tested, I finally managed to say, "No." My answer was barely true. After feeling secure about my honesty, I floundered momentarily wondering if I should say more. "Do I need to explain?"

"No. No, you don't need to explain," he replied. "I don't want to upset you or to delve into things that are none of my business. After all, we just met, and you probably shouldn't go around confiding too much in people you just met. It's just that I can't help being concerned about you. Just answer this: are you safe?"

"That's so sweet," I whispered sincerely. "You don't need to worry about me."

"I know that I could walk out of here and pretend we never met, but I don't want to do that. 'Sides, when I get my Visa bill I'll wonder what the hell I was up to spending double on a dinner alone." He cracked a smile to show me that he was trying to lighten the mood. It didn't work very well. What it did show me, oddly enough, was that he had the potential to understand how my imagination worked. "Is there a reason that I should worry about you, Carmen, whether I have need to or not?"

"No. I'm worried about someone else."

"Oh," and he reached across the table and took my hand. I felt no urge or necessity to draw it away or protest, though I stared at his large, strong hand over the top of mine. He tightened his fingers around mine gently, and I found it pleasant.

Then the waiter returned with the check and the receipts, and Dennis lifted his hand away to take the little vinyl folder. As he jotted numbers and signed for our supper, he asked, "I was wondering if you'd like me to drive you home tomorrow."

"You don't need to…" I began. "I don't mind the bus."

"I was looking for a way to spend more time with you, Carmen." His eyes were fixed on mine.

I looked down at the table top; the cloth had dried completely. "Oh?" I stuttered. I clenched the edge of my seat with both hands, my shoulders high around my ears. "I thought you were planning to stay here for the week." When I dared to look up again, he smiled, his eyes warming.

Patiently he explained, "I'm enjoying your company. We could make the trip more fun for you, and for that I'm willing to miss a day on the beach. I wasn't planning to cut my holiday short. I'll come back to the old Neptune tomorrow night."

"That's a lot of driving for you."

"I don't mind. I like to drive. Besides if I drive you we can make our own schedule. We can take the morning for the beach or take a side trip. You know, make it fun."

"You'll be too tired," I replied, still arguing, stunned by his offer.

In stride, he explained that it was a short trip. "I can do it faster than Greyhound. It will improve my vacation." He looked up with persuasive eyes. "What d'you say, Carmen? Does it sound like fun?"

I don't know what came over me. "Yes," I answered. "It does."

"Really? Oh, that's great." He looked and sounded both happy and relieved. He put his hand across the table again.

Then I broke the mood. "You are a safe driver, aren't you?"

"I think so," he replied. "I can't remember causing any accidents."

"Is that because of all the head injuries you've gotten?"

He looked confused for a moment, and then he grinned. "No."

We wandered through town on our way back. Neither of us was sure if the date would end or continue after we returned to the hotel. He was saying something about walking around the grounds as we went through the revolving doors into the grand lobby. He took my hand again, and we climbed the wide stairway up the center to the mezzanine. I felt proud when I realized that I had not recoiled or stiffened; I was learning to accept this gentle kind of intimacy. I could even feel a certain amount of comfort from the familiarity.

We heard music in the distance, and we followed the sound instinctively out onto the verandah, where there was a band playing. People crowded around the bar and at the dozens of small tables that surrounded the empty dance floor. We stood in the shadows at the edge of the scene. "The band's good," he commented.

"Yeah," I agreed without thinking.

"You want to sit?"

"Not really."

He turned away from the crowd, toward the wall. "I think I'll take a night cruise sometime this week. Out there," he pointed at the glistening darkness of the ocean. "Out where there's no light. You can see the sky so well."

"It's like looking into forever," I said without thinking. Even with the light around us, the sky was beautiful.

He chuckled and very delicately put his hand on my shoulder. "Deep down under there, Carmen, way deep, you've got the heart of a romantic." I disagreed, but I didn't say so. Something told me he would have been insulted if I had. It was too dark for him to see how startled I was. He didn't wait for me to reply. And what could I have said that wouldn't have discouraged our budding friendship? "It's the truth, though, that looking at forever part, I mean. I guess, technically, it's forever into the past, you know, since we are looking very far back in time when we gaze at the stars."

This line of conversation was easier to handle, not that I understood much of it. He had gone all engineery on me, and I liked it. He was treating me as if I were an intelligent and educated woman, and I found it very flattering that he was even a little bit attracted to me. He rambled on for a while about a humble telescope, and I listened more to his pleasant voice than his words.

Then he whispered something about the music I didn't quite catch before he used my name and woke me. Goose bumps rose all down that one side of my body, the oddest sensation. The next thing I knew, he had taken both of my hands and was pulling me away from the wall where we'd been leaning. "I can't let this one pass."

I twitched my shoulders, neither shrugging nor nodding. "I don't know this song."

He drew closer. "My older sister used to play this C.D. all the time. The words were drilled into me almost like the catechism." He stopped talking and maneuvered himself a little closer. He put one of my hands on his shoulder, freeing his for my waist, and we stepped together in what could loosely be termed as dancing. Neither of us trampled the other's toes, and I found myself drawing closer to him within his arms. He touched my cheek lightly with one finger, and I put my other hand on his shoulder. He still held my waist, sometimes with both hands. Never in my life had I experienced anything like this: I was extra alert, but it wasn't from fear. The song changed; the mood did not. Eventually, my cheek rested against his chest, and two of our hands were clasped together in front of my face. We swayed stiffly in time with the music. I felt his cheek resting at the top of my head. I nearly shivered from the heat of the moment. When the music stopped, I lifted my head off of his chest. I didn't know the protocol. I guess he didn't either, because he still held my hands even after we were otherwise separated.

Finally, however, he broke the silence. "Are you tired? Do you want to sit, or go up, or would you like dessert? Or a drink?"

I had already passed through a state of exhaustion. "Yes. I am thirsty."

He took me by the hand and led me to a little, round table with two chairs at the edge of the seating area. I sat, and when he asked me what I'd like, I answered that I didn't know. "What are you having?"

"Champagne?"

I laughed.

"I'll figure something out," he said as he turned to go to the bar.

It was much brighter here near the official dance floor. Paper sheathed lanterns hung on wires overhead, quivering in the ocean air. With no music playing, I could hear the waves crashing in the distance, the bass line running under the murmur of many conversations and the chiming of glassware. I watched Dennis cut through the crowd to the bar until it closed over his path again. I couldn't help smiling at the surprise Father Oleg would be expressing at me if he knew what was going on in my damaged brain. I turned so that I could feel the salt air on my face until I heard the rattle of the metal tabletop when Dennis set down our drinks. He smiled, greeting me anew, as he sat in the other chair. He had moved it around the table partway so that we would be able to hear each other when we talked.

I looked at the two tall, narrow glasses on the table. "What did you get?"

"Taste it."

I lifted my glass and sniffed it. It smelled fruity, but not like alcohol.

Dennis laughed. "It's just soda water and fruit juice."

I tipped it to my lips and slid my tongue into the glass to taste it. Then I took a small sip. "That's nice." I tasted it again, trying to determine what was in it. "Grapefruit?"

"I'm not sure." He tasted his. "Pineapple."

"Orange."

"I don't care. I'll never be able to make it for myself. I don't even know if the bartender can replicate it."

"Which is fine, because I've eaten so much tonight that I should probably have nothing but water for the next couple of days."

"Please tell me you aren't trying to lose weight." When I didn't reply, he held his glass out toward me. I lifted mine, and he clinked his against it. "Cheers!" He leaned back in his seat. "I'm glad you seem to be enjoying yourself, Carmen. It's nice to see you relaxing. I feel like you've been torturing yourself all day, and I confess I'm still a tad worried about you."

"That's very kind, Dennis, but I'm okay."

He didn't look like he believed me. "So, what's your family like? Do you have any brothers and sisters?"

"What?" I stammered, reeling from what he must have thought were innocuous questions. I saw that he was puzzled by my reaction. "Oh," I said as I recovered. "Yes, I have one sister. Joella. She's seventeen."

"Another exotic name. Is she good at this beauty stuff too?"

I shook my head, settling down again. "She doesn't pay much attention to her looks. She's very pretty without doing a thing. She lets her hair go stringy and she doesn't bother with makeup."

"That's good," he began. He stopped, probably afraid of offending me. "At seventeen she shouldn't be too sophisticated." He took a drink, and I wondered if I was supposed to say something. "But you don't look like you're wearing much makeup. When you go to work, do you have to look all glamorous? Like a cover girl?"

I laughed at his notion of me ever looking as good as a model. "Not quite. I'm expected to show our clients how to make the most of their appearance, but we aren't coifing movie stars."

"Bet you still wear high heels all day."

"Usually, but not the really high ones. I'm better at making other people look glamorous."

After another pause he asked, "Have you always wanted to be a beautician?"

"I guess." I shrugged. With some effort, I had managed to uncurl my fingers and toes. "I took some classes in school." I took another drink. It was very refreshing and helped to calm my stomach after my heavy meal. "Did you always want to be an engineer?"

"After I stopped wanting to a fireman. Yeah. I think I developed an interest in the way things worked pretty early on. I was always building models and stuff with Lego." He leaned forward, elbows on the table, but he still seemed content and reflective. "Then I got into cars."

"Real cars? Do you have some kind of fancy sports car?"

"Better. I've got a car I can work on. It's a Pontiac muscle car, older than the two of us put together." His face brightened. "I guess you know you've been hanging out an old guy?"

"I guess." I threw my hand over my mouth. "I mean, I figured you were older than me. But I wouldn't say you are old. You can't be thirty yet?" Then I chastised him, "You know better than to ask such a loaded question. How can I answer it properly?"

"I suppose it wasn't fair. Will you forgive me?"

I shrugged. "Okay." I started the conversation again. "So? What's your family like?"

"Pretty normal. Dad's a civil engineer, Mom's a librarian. My over-grown teeny-bopper sister taught school for a dozen years, and now she's got three kids. My brother does parkour, and my younger sister *lives with* her boyfriend."

I raised my eyebrows. "Scandalous," I said with mock shock.

"Oh, ain't it just?"

"Is that the worst family story you have to tell?"

He blushed. "It's the worst one I know, at any rate—unless you'd like me to make one up."

"I don't know if I should keep talking to you," I joked. I was glad to keep his family as our topic.

"Actually, I think that for them living together is a good idea. Neither of them thinks about the future at all. And I have the feeling that one day one of them may grow up and out of the other one. My folks have accepted it pretty well, and I guess that might be why. Let's just hope they don't have kids, at least not until they mature some more, because kids would tie them together forever."

"You think so?"

"Sure. I mean, who would want to have their children growing up without being there?"

I could think of a few people who might have been content with that arrangement. I said nothing, probably giving him the false impression that I agreed. With a family like his, I might have.

He changed the subject again, perhaps sensing that the topic had become awkward. "You said you liked to play tennis. Would you like to have a game sometime?"

"Sure."

"If you win, I'll buy you lunch. If I win, I'll buy you dinner." He was good at lifting my mood.

"Sounds perfectly fair to me."

"What about swimming? You aren't one of those girls who won't let a man see her in a swimsuit, are you?"

"Better in one than not," I said.

"If you say so, Carmen." Then he added, blushing faster than I did, "I suspect you look good either way."

"I also like bowling," I said quickly.

"There's an alley up in Lofton. Want to go?"

"Now?"

"Sure. It's only." He looked at his cell phone to find the time. "Nine fourteen. Come on. Let's go get a taxi. It'll be fun."

I'm sure that I looked confused for a moment. Then I allowed myself to go with it. This is what I had pledged to do today. "Why not?"

CHAPTER TEN

I looked down at the table, expecting our drinks still to be full and thinking it would be a shame for us to waste them. Somehow between bits of conversation, both of us had drained our glasses. The fizzing fruit juice was refreshing. I felt like moving again, and when we did, I was too busy talking to Dennis to be alert for ghosts.

We got a cab at the front of the hotel. It took us around the headland and up into Lofton, the real town of which the resort of Lofton Beach was only a part. The bowling alley was well-kept and looked more prosperous than the one my friends and I went to in Eastmont. It was busy, but we were able to get an alley and shoes in our proper sizes.

"This is the cleanest bowling alley I've ever been to," Dennis commented. "The food actually looks decent. You hungry?"

"You've got to be kidding." Then I softened my reply, "But don't let me stop you."

"Oh, I don't want anything," he replied. It was apparent that he thought hospitality required the offering of food.

I was entering our names into the scoring computer when I realized that I didn't know his last name, so I asked him what it was.

"Mason. What's yours? Trouble?"

My psyche jumped. I should have known better than to bring up that subject. "How'd you know?" I was glad he made a joke. That gave me a chance to ease into the next stage of the conversation.

"Oh my god! I'm reading your mind now. That's scary!"

If he only knew, I thought. I said, pretending to object, "That's an invasion of my privacy."

"My apologies." He watched me, waiting for my answer.

"It's Trahan." I tried not to change the rhythm of my voice, but the name stuck in my mouth. Now that he knew my family name, I was afraid that he might connect me with the rest of my family. He might have heard about us through other people at church. We didn't live in the same neighborhood, but we could still have acquaintances in common.

My family lived in a rundown rental. My father had been picked up by the police on multiple occasions for public insobriety, minor infractions that had cost him some in fines. I'd had to spend time in the guidance office where they pestered me, trying to get me to accuse my parents of something. They were always trying to sic a social worker on our family again, as if twice hadn't been painful enough. Things were known. Things were guessed. Some things were common knowledge, and now I feared this could have been passed along to my new friend in advance of his meeting me.

"What's the matter?" he asked seeing my face darken.

"It's nothing," I stammered, trying to find something to say that wouldn't bring on more questions.

"Did I say something wrong, Carmen? You look upset. I didn't mean to..."

I lost track of what he said as I thought about the way things had been with my school friends.

"Can't you come in for just a minute, Arlene?"

My friend hesitated on the outside of our screen door. "Are your mom and dad here?" She craned her long neck to look past me into the living room.

"Mom's always here." I saw that she was still hesitating. "My dad's at work. Mom's probably resting. I want to show you what I did in my room. When I was at the thrift shop I got a new bedspread and some other pretty stuff, not just this scarf." I stroked the silk of my first fashion accessory. It was so delicate that I could see through it.

"Oh." Arlene looked torn. Then looking around furtively, she said, "Okay," as she stepped forward to follow me. "It's just my mother doesn't like me going into other people's homes." I knew exactly what she meant. Her mother didn't want her to go into my home; her mother was afraid my parents might treat her the way they treated me or, at the least, treat me the way they usually treated me, revealing things from which most mothers would want to protect their children. I was always welcome in her home, and Arlene wasn't restricted from visiting our other friends. I understood that this was the way things would remain, but I felt alienated by my best friend's slowness to acquiesce and her skittishness was once she was inside.

I would have liked to take her straight to our room without having her see the rest of the house. Though Joella and I kept the rest of the house clean and neat, the furnishings were shabby and the paint was dingy. In our room, we had brightened things a little. We found a nearly full can of bright green paint on the curb for the trash once, and we painted our walls with a kitchen sponge. It was worth the battering it cost; the walls were still bright and the bruises had long since healed. I was proud of the way it looked. I had found newish bedspreads at the thrift shop, and the woman there had given me a discount on some other decorative items because I had donated some of the old, childish things Joella and I wouldn't use any more. It was hard to believe that someone no longer wanted the things I bought that day, they were so nice. I was grateful, though, and I tried not to think about how at a flicker of an impulse my father could destroy our accomplishment. It was a threat that never disappeared.

Jo was straightening her homework papers when we came into the room. She was on her bed, leaning against the colorful stuffed monkey I'd won for her at the Halloween fair at church. The monkey was too large for her to hide from our father, like she did with her favorite toy, a rag doll Aunt Chris had given to her when she was a tot. She had more hiding places than I knew to protect her belongings and her books, even her homework would be tucked away somewhere before Dad came home.

Joella loved books. She read all the time, and because she didn't want to lose her good standing with the library, she only checked out one book at a time. That meant that she went there every two or three days. I was jealous that she had found a way to escape her real life. I wished I had found something that gave me that kind of pleasure.

She looked up and smiled. Once her things were sorted, she got up to leave. Waving as she went out, she said she was going to the library. "I'll be back by five."

"I was hoping to find a new lamp at the thrift shop," I told Arlene. "Hers shorted out a few weeks ago, and she has to read by mine." Jo's nonfunctioning lamp still stood on the top of her dresser beside her bed, and mine was pulled to the full length of its cord to light her schoolwork. Little light came through the window, because of the overgrown bushes, and my lamp was the only source of artificial light.

Arlene tiptoed in behind me. Eyes wide, she looked around, taking it all in, as she had the courtesy not to do until we arrived in this room. She understood things rather well considering I'd never explained my home situation to her. She'd wave to Joella just the way she would to any of our friends' sisters. "I see her just about every time I go to the library, Carmen," she added trying to sound relaxed. She was a good friend, and she would never tell her mother she had been in here. She knew that she was risking her right to spend time with me.

It was like this with all of my friends. They didn't hold things against me. I didn't talk and they didn't ask. We kept things level, but I knew they pitied me, and I resented that pity. It kept us at a little distance. It was easier now that I was grown and my friends didn't need to know about my family. They only needed to know me, and they had no reason to feel sorry for me.

"You're so creative, Carmen," Arlene said with a note of surprise in her voice. I didn't dare to think how she had imagined my room looking, but now that she knew it was not so different from her own, I trusted her to share that knowledge with our other friends. Maybe this was the reason I had longed so very much to share my privacy with the other girls. "I can't believe you found all this at a thrift shop. It looks new."

"Oh, they had scads of newish stuff, Arlene." I took the scarf off and started to fold it.

She admired it again. "It really is gorgeous."

"It goes with everything I own."

She laughed.

I tucked it at the back of the bottom dresser drawer. "Look what the lady at the drug store gave me, Arlene." I held up a two-month old edition of *Glamour* magazine, missing its cover.

Her eyes lit up with anticipation. "Can we take it with us?" She restrained the hand that wanted to reach up and take it from me.

"You bet. I don't want to keep it here. If my mom found it, she'd probably shred it," I whispered.

"I'll keep it for you," she offered eagerly.

"Thanks."

She hid the magazine under her arm and led the way to the front door. I listened at the door to my mother's room for a moment to make sure she was asleep. Though I hadn't thought it was possible that she was awake, I was still relieved to hear her rumbling snores. If she was awake, I would have told her where I was going and when I would return, but it had been months since she had been awake enough for me to feel a need to communicate such things to her.

Once we were outside again, Arlene asked, "Do you always cook dinner?" Perhaps she was letting me know that I could open up to her.

"Yeah. Pretty much every day. Mom's arthritis really bothers her."

"Oh," she said in a leaden tone. Arlene was polite. "Oh, of course, Carmen. I knew that."

I knew Arlene was torn between wanting me to be honest with her about the source of my mother's problem and gratitude that I wasn't. It probably hurt her feelings that I went along with my mother's big lie. It was just that I couldn't admit it, not even in private. It was easier to try to persuade myself that it was really arthritis that kept her in bed all afternoon. It took away the pressures and the guilt of the real situation, which was that she drank so much in the morning, once the rest of us were away for the day, that she couldn't function for hours afterwards. The older I got, the more she drank, the more she slept, the sicker she felt even when she was sober, the less she had to do with Joella and me.

Despite her drinking my mother's wits were still sharp, the liquor seeming only intent upon destroying her body, and except for deluding herself that we didn't know exactly what she was doing, she maintained a tight control over us girls. I don't think anyone could control my father, but she tried. He vexed her so much that to avoid him she drugged herself to sleep again in the evening.

I always had to make sure that I started dinner before Dad came home from work. He rarely did more than stop at the liquor store on the way home anymore; he'd worn out any friendships he might ever have had with his workmates. He was full of resentment, both for the way the other men got along and because he'd been removed from his better paying position on the garbage truck to the sorting shed at the dump. It could have only been kindness or pity that prevented his being fired from the city's public works department, and he probably resented that too, as much as I would have. He stayed sober all day at work. He never had the accidents that his supervisor must have feared he would have. He was irresponsible and heartless, but he had enough self-interest to keep himself out of major trouble.

My father was hard to read. His rugged looks gave him the appearance of health, even up close. His voice gave him away as a heavy smoker, hoarse and spitty, huffing for more air with a persistent throaty cough. Unlike my mother, he looked after his appearance; he combed his hair and shaved and bathed daily. His work was physically demanding, which helped him to maintain a near-healthy weight despite all of the liquor calories. It was my mother who had grown obese.

He gave the impression of moderate friendliness and tolerance. He seemed unremarkable. Yet it would be a mistake to ignore him. His actions were stealthy, like tripping me with the jump rope so I would spill the drinks. He never failed to find ways to catch us off guard. One of his most frequent tricks was to hide something of my mother's in our room with the goal of riling her and enticing her to punish us. Even after she seemed to catch onto this being his trick and restricted her punishments to loud, shrill yelling, he continued for his own amusement, still thinking that it made him seem like the kinder parent. Joella and I knew better, but he never gave up trying the same thing again and again, intelligent enough to become trickier, but not enough to learn the futility of continuing at all.

In a way, it tied us closer to our mother. We could see that she was also a victim of his cruelty. Some part of me believed that she wanted to treat us better, but she didn't seem to care enough about anything anymore to make the effort.

Suddenly I realized what a sad figure she was. My father was not even that. For Joella's future, I could risk his falling into the gutter as he grew older, but I wished it didn't mean dragging my mother down with him. He could take care of himself. Maybe she could too, if she made the right choices, and I finally was able to see that these were her choices to make, not mine.

I blinked, coming back to the present moment. Dennis hovered in front of me, waiting for me to reply to his apology. It was only a moment later, though to me it felt like hours or even years had sped by, bringing me the resolution I needed. The light was behind Dennis, shadowing his face. "Carmen?" he called to me in a whisper, his voice fatigued from repeating himself. "What's wrong?"

I shook my head in an attempt to shed the prickles of my memories. "Dennis," was all I said, as if it were a proper answer.

It seemed enough to tell him that I had returned to the moment I shared with him. "Here. Sit down. Want some water?"

I shook my head.

"Are you ill?" he asked. I imagine that he had already decided that I was mentally ill, and he may have been correct. I was only beginning realize how many feelings and memories I had repressed over my twenty-five years of life.

I shook my head. "It's things, Dennis. Something reminds me of something else, and I've allowed my memories to rise from the grave where I tried to bury them. It's all coming back to me. Today."

"You have some serious problems, don't you?" he asked in a simple summary. I detected no sign of judgment in his voice.

"Yeah. I'm afraid so, Dennis. I was afraid you might have heard about my family, and," I croaked with a failing voice.

"Why? We just met. I don't know anything about your family." His voice was coaxing.

With simple honesty I said, "I owe you an explanation."

"No," he said. "You don't owe me anything. But if it would help you to talk about it, I'd be happy to listen." He knew that 'happy' had nothing to do with what he might hear.

"Dennis." I cleared my throat, fighting the urge to break down and the opposing urge to clam up. "I've tried to remove myself from my family, except for my sister. And I haven't given her half the attention I ought to have. Now she's pregnant, and I've been deciding whether or not to help her."

"Why wouldn't you help your sister?" He looked appalled.

"My mother and father," I began and stopped.

He looked very confused, as I suppose most decent people would be. "Your parents won't help your sister either?" His voice was pitched high and sharp.

"No," I cried sharply, impatient for him to understand this basic truth. "They'll throw her out. So she wants to live with me. But if I take her in and they disown me too, who will take care of them?"

"Can't they take care of themselves, Carmen?" he asked reasonably.

"I don't think so. I don't know. I hope so." Feeling tears rising, I looked down at the floor. "We've always taken care of them, ever since we were old enough. That's the way we were brought up, Dennis: to put them first."

"They sound like child abusers to me, Carmen."

I tried to meet his eyes.

"You poor girl."

It sounded more like sympathy than pity; there is a subtle difference. It didn't hurt my feelings. For the first time in my life I felt like I could tell someone the truth, still the only response I could make was not to deny it, and I said nothing. It was enough. His eyes drew in, warming me, steadying me, allowing me to breathe normally. "I've always felt responsible for them."

"Is it both of them, Carmen?" His head was shaking in denial, finding it terribly difficult to believe that I wanted to protect such faithless people.

"I've decided I will help my sister, Dennis," I said.

It didn't answer his question, but he didn't object. He continued studying me, only moving his eyes. When he saw that I had begun to settle down again, he said, "Joella isn't safe in that home, Carmen. Let's go home, and take her out of there."

"That is what I will do tomorrow."

"Tonight."

"It's too late tonight. She'll be asleep. She'll be okay until tomorrow." Maybe I just wanted to continue postponing action.

He shook his head. He weighed what I had told him along with his own instincts until he finally conceded. "I guess, after this long, tomorrow will be soon enough."

CHAPTER ELEVEN

For the first time that I could remember I gave a prayer of thanks before I slept. The day had been so strange and stressful, but in the evening resolution had brought a type of serenity. I knew that I had been right to trust Dennis. I had promised myself to do something daring this day, and I had continued on that course until I did the bravest thing I may ever have done. I trusted another person, and I accepted his help. Tomorrow I would begin a whole series of brave actions, by confiding in other real people, but I felt prepared. Breaking the news to the real Father Oleg would not be as difficult as anything I had done today.

Dennis was a good person. His concern for me and his reaction when I finally told him the truth were proof enough. As a person who had absolutely no experience dealing with this sort of thing, Dennis had reacted well, calming me and offering simple, logical kindness. For him, it was natural to step in to help other people. Though I was unsure how to deal with having a confidant and accepting his help, I felt that my rescue had begun. Dennis was like a sane answer to the prayers I had never before dared to utter.

I had spotted Father Oleg snoring in comfort on one of the lobby sofas, reminding me of tomorrow's duty. There was no sign of my other apparitions. I managed to shower alone and stretch out in my bed after, pointing my toes, wiggling my fingers, and closing my eyes again and again, finding it harder each time to hold them open as my exhaustion overtook me.

I was going to do the right thing. I would help Joella. She deserved my help. My parents' needs no longer figured into my decision. Despite all of the crazy things that had gone through my head and my throat, I began to feel that I had always known this was the right choice to make. My fictional version of Father Oleg had asked me why I wouldn't help my sister, but it took hearing that question from a real person, someone whose ideas and opinions came from outside of my brain, for me to see the black and white of what was truly a bloody, red mess.

In my dreaming I sifted through much of today's mind fodder until I absorbed it in my marrow. I felt a kind of contentment. I knew that I had stepped into a new phase of my life. I would never again have such a day as this one; from now on I would be working with my sister toward solutions for our problems.

And my dreams shifted, suggesting that there could be other good things in my future.

I was again dancing with Dennis. He held my hand cradled in his own while I leaned my head against his shoulder. His shirt felt smooth, like the sheet under my cheek. His other hand supported my back, and he began to stroke it gently at first, adding pressure and arousing me. I arched my neck, reaching for an elusive kiss. His hand slid up my back to my scalp, and then his fist closed around some of my hair. His other hand slid down my front to part my thighs, opening them with unexpected urgency. He twisted my hair until my scalp was pulled taut, yanking my neck back hard.

Even asleep, I became confused. I couldn't figure out why Dennis would treat me in such a rough and impatient way. I tensed, withdrawing, feeling ill at ease, but he pulled me closer, roughly turning my body so that my back was to his front. The scent of whiskey and a long day's sweat assaulted my nose, and I understood that this man was not Dennis. I was waking, but I was still held captive. Memories had replaced dreams.

I moved my arms protectively in front of my body. His whiskers scratched my cheek in rhythm with the motion of his body. He panted and grunted as he pleasured himself against my hip and thigh, his calloused fingers rooting about in the sensitive area between my legs. I felt the urge to urinate as my muscles tightened. There was no point in asking to be released to use the toilet. He didn't care if I wet my bed. He probably would have found it amusing and used it against me.

I knew the rules. I was not to get out of bed at night for any reason. While my father was with me, I had to keep silent. I pressed my lips together, biting down into the flesh to keep from releasing sound. My father grunted and made the bed squeak. As always, I was too frightened not to obey. I knew in my soul that I would be right to protest and that I did what I understood to be wrong because experience had taught me that it would hurt less to submit than to rebel. My mother wouldn't have protected me from him, even if I had been able to convince her that these things had happened. In our perverted home, it was safest to comply with any request. I had never been in a position to do otherwise.

Reliving an event from the depths of my buried memories, I was held there just as completely as I had been as a small girl, unable to draw my mind away. It seemed real, three-dimensional, bruising, and stinking. Every sensation was replayed.

My father grabbed my wrists and forced me to turn to face him, for he did to me only what stimulated him, and he found limited stimulation in poking fingers into tight spaces. As usual, I was almost relieved to move on to the next stage in this dreadful series of acts, wanting to rush ahead to the point when I could roll up into a tight, little ball and try to forget. He put my hands where he wanted them to go, moving them to set the pace for me. He grunted into my ear, "Faster." I obeyed. He put his hands on either side of my face and pushed me down lower against his body. I gasped, and he swatted my scalp. He was always careful not to leave bruises where they could be seen, probably so that my mother would think that she was the only one who had given in to violence. I knew what he wanted. We were coming near the end, and then, I reminded myself, he would leave me alone. Still I had to pretend that I was getting ready to suck on a massive lollipop, but it seemed more like the body of a hot squid—still better than what really went into my mouth. He never trusted me to take it in completely or quickly enough, so he thrust it in with a force that made me gag. His fingers pressed into my skull, but he allowed my head to move enough to give him pleasure. For a few minutes he had to give me some control. If he didn't, I couldn't make him happy. For a little while before his time came, I didn't gag.

Tonight, however, he was more restless or angry than usual. He forced my face in deeper, faster, harder, making my mouth move up and down on him. I felt vomit rising from my gut. I resisted, and he pushed harder. He was too large, too strong, too cruel. My revulsion overrode my trained responses. I clamped my jaws as hard as I could onto his erect penis.

For an instant I felt victorious. I had hurt him. He wouldn't want to risk it happening twice. So his laughter struck me doubly hard. That low chuckle should have been spontaneous, but it was contrived to humiliate me. It was also one of the happiest sounds I had ever heard the man make.

He shoved my face into his genitals, smothering me, even as his organs moved with his laughter, not softening or shrinking. My bite had done little more than pinch him. My little top teeth were neither large enough nor sharp enough to even scratch him, especially with the two lower center ones missing altogether. I could hardly bite into my cooked and dead supper; how had I thought to fend off a strong and living man?

I think his amusement stemmed more from this evidence of his unrestricted power over me than anything I had done to him thus far. His mucosal mess came quickly after. Grumbling that I'd brought him along too quickly, he slugged me hard in the crotch, and then he was done save for a few final pants, grunts, and belches.

He rolled over and swung his feet to the floor. I coiled immediately, but before I caught my breath after his final blow, he grabbed my buttocks, one in each big, clumsy hand, and squeezed hard. "Don't you ever fucking bite me again, you little pisser. You're damn lucky those teeth haven't grown in yet or I'd have knocked them out!"

I listened, silent and alert.

"Swear it," he demanded in a husky, strained voice. He couldn't blame his behavior on the liquor. Its effects had worn off, and he was sober.

"Yes, Daddy, I promise. I won't try to bite you again."

He took half the covers with him when he rose, wiping himself dry on the sheet before he left the room. I couldn't wait to turn over to face the wall opposite the door again, pulling my nightgown down tight over my knees and finally curling into as small a ball as I could make. I didn't want to have the covers over me; I needed air; I needed to be unrestrained. In the morning my mother would rant at me yet again about the strangeness of my sleep habits when she saw that my bed was torn apart and I was balled up and cold when she woke me for school. I would lie to her again, saying that I must have gotten hot while I was asleep.

In the meantime, I lay awake for a long time, longing to rise, to wash, to run away from home, and afraid of being caught, sure that the punishment would be even worse than the things I had already endured. I couldn't leave my baby sister behind either, though I couldn't have taken her with me, and as much as I wanted to leave my mother, I sensed that she needed me. Eventually I would sleep again, for tired children truly do need the rest and tortured people need the escape. I convinced myself that I had had another very bad dream.

But this night, in the present, I had awakened in order to remember and unlock the truth. I lay on my cold hotel bed in a tight ball, my knees burrowed into the shirt of my pajamas, as terrified as I had been after one of my father's nocturnal visits.

I shivered as much from all my various fears as from the cold of my exposed, sweat-dampened flesh. Bringing these memories to my active mind forced me to deal with what I had trained myself to forget: all those memories I had blocked each day with greater strength from year to year so that I could make it from one day to the next as a decent human. Always I had feared that a word about my father's incestuous practices would have brought on worse punishment. As a child I had believed that there could always be something worse, a belief that I am certain my father encouraged in me, for all it would have taken was one word from me to ruin his hellish life. That my mother might have believed me or defended me from him never seemed possible. A woman who treated her children the way she treated Joella and me did not fill those children with confidence and trust, and yet their training to distrust other people held no matter how badly we were broken by our parents.

As I grew older I did my best to put his nocturnal visits behind me. I pretended they had never happened until I believed they had not. I put it all far back in my past, like babyhood, beyond my memories. Only this wasn't something I could completely forget. This memory had followed the others out of my brain's Pandora's box.

Suddenly, I sat up, gasping, "Joella! Oh, my God, Joella!" Could my father have turned to my younger sister for his pleasures? Could he have sought her bed once mine was empty? Could he still be tormenting her? "Dear God! Could he be the father of her child?"

I could barely breathe through the tension. Unnoticed, tears drained from my eyes and sweat through my pores.

Then the other fear, the fear of speaking out, returned. I started to balk, to try to push my memories away again because they were too horrible and the possibilities were too disgusting, but now that I had opened my mind, I had to acknowledge them. Still I thought of my mother and wondered how to protect her from this newly exhumed truth.

Yet, what good would it do to continue hiding it from her? What good had it ever done?

None. Absolutely no good had come from perpetuating the lies.

And more important even than shielding my mother was doing right by Joella.

It was time for me to face the consequences of my choice to keep silent. If I had suffered less as the years passed, it was likely that Joella had been made the victim in my stead, and that made me one of the guilty parties. I had left her alone in that home knowing that my father might molest her and that my mother would beat her. I knew and chose to ignore that Joella might end up suffering doubly without me to deflect some of the attention.

I knew the answer, of course. There were nights when I had heard the noises on her side of the room. I heard her cry after, and I had pretended to believe her when she told me she had had nightmares. If I had asked more questions, she might have explained. We might have joined together, worked together, helped each other, but we were separated from each other by what we shared, neither one wanting to admit that she had accepted this sinful role. We were ashamed, and that shame was the wall that held us imprisoned apart.

At last, admitting the truth with my waking mind, I could no longer shove it away from my consciousness. For Joella's sake, I had to preserve these foul memories. Worse, terrible and terrifying as it was, I needed to tell someone what had happened to us. There was no protection, no safety in our parents' home, but I could make sure Joella had a safe place to go.

I felt certain that she had faced worse than I, that our father had raped her. She had wanted to tell me, but I had barely listened to her when she tried to open up to me. She needed far more help than I could give to her, and she needed guidance through far more complex issues.

I knew what I needed to do, but when I looked at the clock I hesitated. This had gone on so long. Must I wake people in the middle of the night? Maybe I should have, but I held back. I needed an intermediate step, a practice for the real revelation. I got up and made ready to have another visit with the imaginary Father Oleg Fuentes.

CHAPTER TWELVE

I ran down the hall to the stairs, flying down them blindly, careless of my safety. I went to the bottom of the stairwell before I realized I had gone too far. More slowly, I climbed back up to the level of the lobby. There were people in the lobby, staff at the desk and crews cleaning the vast public spaces. I ran past them looking desperately for Father Oleg.

He emerged from the shadows in the central part of the lobby where I had last seen him peacefully asleep. He was coming toward me, but I darted across the distance so quickly that he had barely moved from his couch before I reached him. He spread his arms, and I nearly fell into them, but I stopped short, remembering just in time that he was not a real person who could keep me from falling if I trusted him to support my weight. I had so much wished never to call him to my mind again, but I still needed him.

"Carmen." His voice wrapped around me the way his phantom arms could not. His eyes moved slowly, blinking catlike at the light. I couldn't pretend that he didn't know exactly what I knew, but I had come here to put my memories into words, to practice for a later time when I would tell Father Oleg or some other counselor, someone who did not already know my thoughts.

He waited for me. I didn't do anything. Well, I guess, I was breathing, probably fast and shallow.

"Tell me what's happened," he said, trying to open the conversation.

Now that it was my turn to talk, I couldn't speak. I could have screamed, but I managed not to.

He just watched me. Silent and patient. He sat down.

I sat beside him and wedged my hands between my knees, palm to palm. I stared into my lap. My eyes stung. Oleg, remembering how I had reacted to his touch earlier, wedged his hands between his knees too, with his head down while his eyes slid sidewise to watch me. I couldn't have been more keenly aware of his presence if he were dancing and singing in front of me.

"Sorry," I said at length. It was very quiet. He didn't react, so he may not have heard me. "Sorry I woke you, Father." It came out louder on the second try.

"Well, I'm sure you have a good reason." He yawned cheerfully.

I still hesitated to speak, but I couldn't hold back my tears. They were warm on my cheeks, but they didn't heat my body. I guess my anger had a flow direction now, so it didn't burn through me the way it usually did.

"Take your time, Carmen," he said. "No pressure. I know you have something you need to say, and I'll wait until you are ready to say it." He sat quietly, urging me out of my silence. "I'll wait until it's time for you to check out and meet your bus."

"Actually," I said, warming my voice. "I'm going to ride back to Eastmont with Dennis. He drove a car here."

"Oh?" He looked at me more carefully, arching his eyebrows and making a circle with his mouth. "Is that a good idea?"

"I hope so. I mean, he seems okay. I trus-trust him."

"You're sure?" He was still watching me. "Your date went well?"

"It did. I won't need to eat for another week, but I had a good time. I was up a little late, and I went to bed happy." I smiled. I much preferred to discuss this than what I had come to discuss.

"Alone? You haven't come to brag about your romantic conquests, have you? I don't think I want to know about that."

"What?" I reacted before he finished speaking. My mind had turned aside for a minute, and then I remembered. "Yes," I said tersely, "I went to bed alone. All alone. No imaginary people even. It was nice."

"So why aren't you still there?"

"My privacy was invaded," I answered hoarsely after too long a break.

"Alone in your hotel room? Was it the telephone or one of your fantasies?"

"All day my visions have invaded my space."

"Hey!" he cried defensively. "You invited us!"

"I know." I drummed on my lap, slugging my fists into my thighs. "I know I did. And I started something. My nightmares came alive too." My breath tightened. "It was so real, Father. It was like he was there, with me, in my bed."

"Who? Dennis?"

"It started as Dennis." I smiled. "I think that made it worse. I went from feeling happy and trusting, and when it changed it almost took away my trust in every man."

"Me too?"

"You? Well, you're not really a man."

"Not me the daydream, but the original me is."

"I don't think so," I replied to his first question, and he didn't further defend his masculinity. "I still trust Dennis. And Robert, but he's not involved in this."

"Okay. So go on. I take it Dream Dennis didn't stick around to protect you from the nightmare?"

"No. My dream shifted, and everything shifted over into waking nightmare."

"That's good. I mean, you still like Dennis in your subconscious?"

"Right."

"So who was in the nightmare?"

"My father."

He took a long, shallow breath, then sat silently, poised to hear more. "Your father?"

"My father."

"You mean that sly bastard actually got his own hands dirty? I thought he just riled your mother to beat you."

"When she was awake, it was all about upsetting her and pushing her to punish us. But when she didn't know what was going on, he did whatever he wanted. He was never too lazy to hurt us. He just didn't want her to know that he stooped below her level."

"What did he do to you?"

"What he always did, Father."

"What was that, Carmen? You need to say it. If you can't tell me, how will you protect Joella?"

Words rushed to my lips. I wanted them to pass out from my mouth without having to hear or taste them, but that was impossible. "He made me give him oral sex."

"Is that all?"

"All?" I objected. "Isn't that enough?"

"It is more than enough, Carmen. I just want to know if there was more. He did more to you, didn't he?"

"That was the worst of what he did to me. He used to come to my bed after everyone else was asleep, and he'd wake me up by touching me. He'd make me part my legs. I tried to stay rolled up on my side for as long as I could, even pretending to sleep. He never bought it."

"I see. And I don't suppose he cared that he woke you?"

"Well, he had to. Who can give a blow job in her sleep?"

"He never had coitus with you?"

"No."

He studied me carefully. "That you've remembered anyway."

"I'm sure, Father. I'm a virgin."

"Really? Interesting."

"I've got a little intimacy issue," I confessed.

"I hadn't noticed," he said, barely controlling an edge of sarcasm in his tone. He didn't mean it to be insulting, and I didn't protest. He was the one who had brought that pearl of truth to my attention. "And your sister? Do you think he's been doing this with her since you moved away?"

I nodded, new tears starting in my eyes, mixing with the old tears on my cheeks. "Now that I remember what happened to me, I remember that he went to her too. I heard them. She never said anything to me."

"Even before you left home? Do you know what he did with Joella? You shared a room, right?"

"We did. It woke me. She cried and he grunted." I shook my head, blaming myself over again. "I was relieved that he was spending time with her. Isn't that wicked? I hoped that he preferred a younger girl. That he would stop coming to me."

Oleg's head shot up as he turned to me again. "A younger...how old were you? When did this happen?" He couldn't keep the look of disgust from his face. Each bit of new knowledge seemed more difficult for him to accept.

"I'm not sure exactly when it started, Father. It's been as long as I can remember."

"You mean, like, before Joella was born?" His eyes, searching my face, saw the answer. "You were only seven when she was born. How old were you in tonight's memory?"

"Joella was only a few months old. I'd just lost my first teeth. And I tried to bite him. I guess I was in second grade."

Neither of us said anything for a long time. The staff worked on the other end of the lobby, trying to give me privacy or wanting to avoid the crazy girl who talked to the sofa as if she saw someone sitting in it. Time dragged. I yawned. Oleg looked my way again. "Carmen?"

"Hmm?" I began to step my feet forward and back, left up, left back, right up, right back, pacing where I sat. I had to keep my blood flowing. I had to burn energy.

"When did it stop? Did he switch over to Joella and leave you alone?"

"Oh?" I tried to sit up straighter now that we were talking again. "No. I don't know how often he went to Joella, but he didn't stop coming to me."

He prodded me gently. "When was the last time, Carmen?"

"One a.m. on the fourteenth of July seven years ago. I'd already started moving my things out of the house."

He showed no shock that I could answer him so precisely. In fact, he seemed to have expected that type of answer and would have been disappointed by any less specific response. Then after a deep breath, he asked, "Is it possible that he is the father of Joella's baby?"

I crossed myself. "I hope not. What do we do if he is?"

"What do you think you should do?"

"Would he be arrested?"

"Probably. Don't you want him to be arrested and go to prison?"

"I don't know." I turned to him. "I forget sometimes that you aren't really Oleg Fuentes."

"You aren't really losing your mind, are you, Carmen?"

"I hope not." I wiped my cheeks with the palms of my hands. "I know I'm a mess right now, but I feel like I had to come apart a little before I can put things back together."

"That makes sense."

"You think I should get some therapy?"

He nodded his agreement. "You seem ready. That should help. Don't be afraid to ask for help. I mean real help."

I said nothing for a while. I had gone through so much in such a short time that I had to work to remember how my day had started. "I feel like I'm riding the crest of a tsunami," I observed.

"Amen." Then it was his turn to think. At last he asked, "Are you going to get Father Oleg involved? I'm sure he could help you handle this."

I nodded. "I'm going to call first thing in the morning. I won't wake him up in the middle of the night."

"I'm sure that would be alright with him."

"Maybe, but it's not necessary. I've waited all this time. What will a few hours mean?"

"Do you think that Joella's in immediate danger?"

I shrugged again. "No more than usual, I suppose, unless they found out that she was pregnant."

"In which case..." He didn't need to complete that particular thought. "Will you be able to sleep again, Carmen?"

"I doubt it."

"I'll stay up with you as long as you want to talk."

I looked around the lobby, wondering how attentive the hotel's caring employees were. I couldn't tell, which made me wonder how often they encountered this type of strange behavior. I didn't think they were ready to call an ambulance for me. I let out a sigh, relieved to have completed this phase of the process. The other parts of this conversation needed to take place in the offices of the police, the church, and a licensed therapist. Some of them needed to include Joella, and they needed to begin soon. I was ready to try to rest.

"I'm okay for now, Father," I said with more confidence than I would have believed possible an hour before. "If I don't sleep, I will at least rest." I felt that I would be ready to call the church at the first humane hour of the morning. I was sure that the real Father Oleg would know exactly what needed to be done to protect my sister, and there was nothing more important than that.

"Good night, then, my girl. I think I'll head back to the rectory now since I'm awake. You and Dennis deserve to have some time alone on your trip home."

"Thanks. Good night." I stood.

Smiling at me he rose and walked stiffly, leaning more heavily than ever on his cane. I watched until he disappeared through a closed glass door, then I slowly walked to the elevator and rode it back up to my room.

CHAPTER THIRTEEN

Relief was in sight, but once I reentered my room so was that bed. And I knew the instant I saw it that I wasn't going to return to it again that night. Like the twin mattress of my childhood, there were monsters around it that attacked at night. Unlike my childhood bed, however, I had no requirement to sleep there.

I moved the table from between the two big, fake leather chairs, and drew one to the other so that I could, still dressed, lay down on them, head in one, feet in the other. I wrapped myself in my beach towel and curled up in this new nest. I didn't expect to sleep, but I thought that I could relax and turn my thoughts forward. I was too restless. I squirmed and began tapping my toes in rhythm with my quickening respiration until I popped up, grabbed my room key, and flew back down the stairs to the third floor where there was an exit to the verandah where I'd found a moment of contentment before I went to dinner.

It was peaceful outside, quieting. Gradually, my breath slowed and my thoughts stopped nagging me. The darkness snugged around me. Without thought or plan, I knelt on a bench and leaned against the parapet, listening for the sounds of the ocean. I could hear the surf clearly without the competing sounds of the day, and it lulled me. I stayed conscious just long enough to lower myself onto the bench.

I slept a blessed sleep, dreamless and sweet.

It was light when I woke, and I drifted back to sleep again and again, until I noticed that I was tucked inside a lightweight blanket. The blanket was real; some hotel employee on patrol had seen to my comfort unbidden. The smell of breakfast, bacon and coffee, was real, and so was the hunger I felt. I rolled carefully onto my side, disengaging my arms and legs from the excess cloth, and began to rise. I was fully awake, amazingly refreshed, and ready for my day to begin, though I was afraid of ruining it the moment I returned to my room. I checked my watch. It was a quarter 'til seven, and I decided I had time to eat a little something before I pushed myself to make the telephone call I dreaded as much as I desired.

I caught my reflection on the chrome around the entry to the coffee shop. If I had thought about it, I would have assumed that I would look a mess, but I didn't. I must have slept so soundly that I hadn't mussed my hair in the least since I'd combed it before going to the lobby in the middle of the night.

I ordered toast and a cup of coffee with a large portion of skim milk, hoping to get alertness from one and calm from the other. I was done in moments, far from lagging over my food as I usually did.

I blocked my peripheral vision with my hands and plowed past the bed to the desk where my purse was. I got out my phone and searched the internet for The Church of Holy Mercy in Eastmont. I wrote down the telephone number. My mouth was dry, so I went to the bathroom and brushed my teeth. I felt much more prepared after that, but still I felt my throat tightening as I dialed. I told myself that I just needed to ask for Father Oleg. I could even pretend I was calling the imaginary one if I needed to keep up my courage.

I didn't know when the church office opened, so I called the school. A woman answered, and I was relieved that she didn't ask my name before she paged Father Oleg. The way my voice shook had probably warned her to skip the social courtesies.

No sooner did she place my call on hold than I heard his voice. I couldn't imagine how he could have gotten to the phone so quickly. "This is Father Oleg Fuentes." It was his real voice, pitched just a mite higher than I had remembered.

"Father Oleg, this is Carmen Trahan." My voice shook.

"Hello, Carmen." He spoke at a measured pace. "I'm glad to hear from you. How are you?" He used his prayer voice. I was sure that he knew I was in trouble.

I wanted to hang up the telephone. I wasn't ready yet, I thought. My jaw quivered, my resolve weakened, and my voice hung off a cliff, pedaling like a cartoon villain, unable to speak. He waited for me. Surely he had gotten this kind of call before, especially on a Monday morning, early. He knew that I had some great need. As a sob escaped my throat, I heard him try to say something. I couldn't understand him. At last I caught my breath and swallowed. Tears blinded me. "I need." I couldn't make myself get any closer to the real issue.

"Where are you, Carmen?"

"Lofton Beach. I'm in a hotel."

"Which hotel are you in? What's your room number?" he asked briskly.

"Neptune. 527."

"Take your time and tell me everything."

"I'll try," I said. "I can hardly talk. But, I trust you as I trust no other person, Father. I need your help. I need you to help my sister."

"Of course, Carmen," he replied without even a pause to consider what I might ask of him. It didn't matter. He was willing, and that was why I trusted him so much. "Tell me what's going on."

"It's Joella, Father," I choked and swallowed. "I'm worried about Joella. Can you make sure she's gets to school today? That she's safe?" I didn't wait for him to answer, but I think he was silent. I could picture him listening and trying not to throw any obstacles into my path now that I was opening up to him. "She's pregnant, and my mother beats her, and my father," I gulped. "Well, my father—"

He waited for me to finish. He knew I had to say it. When I didn't finish, he prodded me. "Carmen? What about your father?"

"He—oh—what if he's the father of her baby?" The words rushed, stumbling out of my mouth. I couldn't believe he could understand them through the clatter. "He is a sexual abuser," I said more clearly and repeated those ugly words to gain confidence. "He is a sexual abuser."

"What did she tell you?" he asked, stunned I guessed by the seriousness of this accusation.

"Nothing. I mean, she told me she was pregnant and that the baby's father is her boyfriend, Justin. She didn't say anything about our father doing this to her. Never a word. She just asked me if she could move in with me. Because she can't stay with them. I know about the abuse because, you see, he did it to me, and I am certain that he has done the same to her. Only worse." I felt I owed an explanation to him for why I had said nothing before. "I've spent this weekend forcing…I have forced these memories to come back to me. I had to remember to help her, but I didn't want to remember."

"I see. Yes, this is difficult. You don't need to explain anything more now, Carmen. I promise you your sister is safe. Are you ready to come back? I can send someone to get you."

"No. I'll take the bus." Then I thought of Dennis with the car. Suddenly the thought of riding with him sounded so good to me. "Well, I might be able to get a lift. I'm coming back today as early as I can get there."

"Come straight here, Carmen, to the church. Do you understand?"

"Yes. I will." I nodded to the telephone. "But Joella?"

"She's—"

"Father! Can't someone go after her?"

"Carmen, listen to me." He forced his voice inside my head. "Joella is safe. She is here at the church."

"What?" I trusted him, but not my hearing.

"We took Joella in on Friday. After she talked to you, she went back to her school and saw her guidance counselor. She thought that she had asked too much of you. The counselor got things started for her, and she called us. I've talked to Joella. A couple of our sisters took her to see a doctor. She's staying here with them for now, and I think you should too. Come here and stay with your sister and sort through all of this together."

"I was going to see her tonight…" I began helplessly.

"She told us that."

"I let her down," I said, sinking into distress again.

"No, Carmen. You did not let her down," he said loudly and firmly.

"I've let her down all of her life."

"No, you haven't, Carmen. You've been the best sister to her that you knew how to be. And I know you can't see it yet, but you have helped her a great deal already with this problem. You got her to ask for our help, Carmen. We are trained to handle this sort of thing. And Joella understands that you have confused feelings about your family. So does she. She doesn't blame you. She was upset, actually, that she might have been unfair to you by asking for help from you the way she did."

I wept.

He must have sensed it, because his voice became very gentle. "Carmen? I need you to talk to me, my dear."

"Okay," I said.

"You said you might have a ride. When will you know?"

"I think I should just take the bus."

"I want you to take the ride or to take one that I find for you. I want you to be comfortable. And you need privacy. I can get someone from a church in Lofton to fetch you."

"The bus is okay."

I could picture him shaking his head at me, a small echo of yesterday's mood. It told me that I knew better than to disregard his advice. "Carmen? Do you have a friend there with you?"

"Well. I met this guy yesterday. He used to go to your church."

"Who is it?"

"Dennis Mason. Do you know him?"

"Yes. I know him."

"He drove here."

"How'd you meet Dennis?" he asked. It seemed like a strange question, but maybe he wanted me to ease back from the tough stuff for a while.

"I was having trouble getting my door unlocked. He offered to help. Then he sat with me at lunch."

"So he's right at the same hotel? That's great."

"I'm supposed to meet up with him at eight."

"To tell him you want to take the bus?"

"It's a long drive he doesn't need to make."

"I don't think he'll mind," Father Oleg said. "Dennis is a good sort."

"Is he a safe driver?"

He chuckled quietly. "Hell, if I know, Carmen. But I think that he is a safe person, if you know what I mean. He'll understand that it's important for you to get here in one piece."

"I don't want to put him out."

"Okay. Well, let me ask you: how is it you think he might give you a ride?"

"He offered to bring me back today."

"He offered? Well, then you don't have to worry about putting him out."

"But if I'm coming home now instead of later like we planned…"

"Does he have any idea what is going on with you, dear girl?" Father Oleg asked in a tender voice. He waited a few moments, for me to answer, and when I did not, he said, "He won't mind."

Father Oleg had tears in his eyes later that morning when I saw him. He hugged me tight against his chest the way a father is supposed to hold a child. He was only about forty-five years old, but at that moment he could have been two thousand.

And Joella met my eyes. I didn't want to meet hers, but she ducked low so that her face blocked my view of my toes.

"Everything will be better now, Carmen," she said. She was sure. She took my hand and held it against her smooth cheek. "This baby is Justin's, and I'm scared but happy about having it, no matter how things work out. We've loved each other very much."

"But Dad?"

"Dad kept away from me ever since I shoved one of his balls into the bulb socket of my lamp that time." I was at a loss, so she explained. "I was about eight. Dad had been coming to me a lot, even more than he went to you. So for a few nights I slept with my lamp in the bed. It was turned on, but I took the bulb out. And when he came to me I kept it hidden, secret, until he wanted me to suck on him." She made a face. "And I spit on his little jewels and plugged him in. Broke the lamp." After a breath, "Dad stayed away from me after that."

"Completely?"

"He found other ways to hurt me. But they weren't as bad."

I felt weak. I sat down on the sofa and shifted my eyes around the church parlor. "Joella." I started to laugh and cry, humor and torment together. "You are magnificent!"

"I should have helped you, Carmen." She settled in beside me and put her arm around my still rocking shoulders. "However, I could use a few favors now."

"Of course, Joella. I've decided that the future and the present are more important than the past. I may not approve of your having a baby, but it would be wrong if I made things more difficult for you."

"Thank you," she said soberly.

"What I went through this weekend, Joella..." I didn't know how to continue. "We have finally been brought together, and I don't want us to come apart again. Not like we were. We have to talk to each other."

"I'll promise if you'll promise," Joella said cheerfully, wiping her nose with the back of her hand. "Aunt Chris and Uncle Howard want us to stay with them for a while."

"In Charleston? I have to work, Jo," I protested.

"Just for a while."

"But I thought you wanted to move in with me." I was stuck in the place I had been unwilling to go until last night. "You can stay with me," I replied, sniffling.

"Thank you, Carmen." She squeezed my shoulders and kissed my cheek. "I hope we'll be able to do that. Eventually." She patted my hand. "For now, though, I think we need more than just each other. We should be around other people and learn how civilized families behave. We have so much to learn if we are going to live happy lives."

"Happy lives…" I echoed numbly.

"Who would have seen us Friday and thought we'd be like this today, Carmen?" She was cheerful. "I have hope. We'll get Mom into treatment, and Dad may get what he deserves. No matter what, he won't be able to hurt you again." Her confidence made me feel hope too. I reached out to her, and she took me into her arms. I allowed her to hold my weight and let her kiss my hair. "I'll share what I've learned of love with you, Carmen. It is the best place to start."

I threw what belongings I had taken out of my bag into it after I washed my face again. I figured it was pretty much pointless to waste any time trying to look less wretched. Just as I pulled closed the zipper on my duffel bag, there was a knock at my door. My watch showed nearly eight o'clock. I wasn't sure if I hoped it was Dennis or a maid offering to clean my room early. If I'd known more about hotels, I wouldn't have thought for a moment that it could be anyone other than Dennis.

He moved slowly, stiff with sorrow. He almost reached out to hug me, but when he saw that my strength was too fragile yet to rest he took hold of my hands instead. It was enough, and I felt better, strong enough for a few more hours.

"Father Fuentes called me," he said. "He said you needed to get home right away. I'm ready to leave now. Are you?"

"Yes," I replied. "I am ready."

The End